Billy Buckhorn
ABNORMAL
by Gary Robinson

7th Generation
Summertown, Tennessee

7th Generation, an imprint of
Book Publishing Company
PO Box 99, Summertown, TN 38483
888-260-8458
bookpubco.com
nativevoicesbooks.com

ISBN: 978-1-939053-07-7
19 18 17 16 15 14   1 2 3 4 5 6 7 8 9

Library of Congress Cataloging-in-Publication Data

Robinson, Gary, 1950-
Billy Buckhorn : abnormal / Gary Robinson.
pages cm. -- (Billy Buckhorn supernatural adventures ; 1)
ISBN 978-1-939053-07-7 (pbk.)
ISBN 978-1-939053-94-7 (e-book)
1. Cherokee Indians--Oklahoma--Fiction. [1. Cherokee Indians--Fiction. 2. Indians of North America--Oklahoma--Fiction. 3. Supernatural--Fiction. 4. Healers--Fiction.] I. Title. II. Title: Abnormal.
PZ7.R56577Bi 2014
[Fic]--dc23

2014003787

Billy Buckhorn's story begins in *Abnormal* and continues in *Paranormal* and *Supranormal*. Watch for these further volumes in the Billy Buickhorn Supernatural Adventures series, coming soon!

Book Publishing Company is a member of Green Press Initiative. We chose to print this title on paper with 100% postconsumer recycled content, processed without chlorine, which saved the following natural resources:

• 30 trees
• 938 pounds of solid waste
• 14,023 gallons of water
• 2,586 pounds of greenhouse gases
• 14 million BTU of energy

For more information on Green Press Initiative, visitgreenpressinitiative.org. Environmental impact estimates were made using the Environmental Defense Fund Paper Calculator. For more information visit papercalculator.org.

CONTENTS

ACKNOWLEDGMENTS

I would like to thank Jesse and Sandy Hummingbird for reviewing this manuscript and contributing to the development of this book. They provided useful feedback regarding the way aspects of Cherokee culture and medicine practices are used.

I also want to thank my best friend and significant other, Lola, for her love and support in all things. She has been by my side for more than ten years. I love and appreciate her so much. No words printed here could really express my true feelings, but I couldn't do this work without her with me.

NOTE TO READERS

O-si-yo (hello). Please note that this is a work of fiction. However, in the interest of realism, I've blended true elements of Cherokee culture and history with made-up tribal culture and history. Some parts have been adapted to protect the secrecy of certain medicine practices and ceremonies. Others have been invented to create a more interesting and dramatic story. I point this out so some critical readers won't dismiss the book because it lacks accuracy. And so that other people won't think I am revealing Cherokee cultural secrets incorrectly. *Wa-do* (thank you).

—*Gary Robinson*

abnormal: (ab-*nor'* mel) *adj.* unusual; unnatural; not normal

CHAPTER 1
Summer's End

The muggy August air clung to Billy Buckhorn's Cherokee skin like a wet blanket. He and his best friend, Chigger, were night fishing on Lake Tenkiller in eastern Oklahoma. This region, part of the old Cherokee Nation, was filled with rivers, creeks, and lakes. All nestled between heavily wooded hills.

"Drop that light down closer to the water," Billy said in a loud whisper.

Chigger let out a few more inches of rope until the camping lantern almost touched the water's still surface.

"How's that?" he asked.

"Just fine," sixteen-year-old Billy replied.

Chigger, also sixteen, tied off the rope and picked up his fishing pole.

Night fishing was one of Billy's favorite things to do in the summer. Well, really, he liked fishing any time of day or night, any time of year. And hunting, too, for that matter. He liked Cherokee bowhunting the best. Billy had learned these skills from his Cherokee grandfather, Wesley.

From somewhere off in the murky distance along the lake's shoreline, the boys heard the snap of a breaking branch and a rustling of leaves.

"What was that?" Chigger whispered nervously. Unlike Billy, he wasn't such a big fan of night fishing. Or doing much of anything at night that involved being outside in the dark. But he'd follow Billy anywhere, anytime.

"Probably just a possum or badger hunting for food," Billy replied calmly.

Chigger picked up a flashlight from the seat next to him. Turning it on, he pointed its beam in the direction the sound came from. A pair of glowing red eyes peered back at him from the lake's edge

"What the—!" Chigger exclaimed with a jump, dropping the flashlight into the lake.

"Not so loud," Billy demanded, as he watched the light sink out of sight. "Now look what you've done."

"There was somethin' evil-looking over there watching us!" the scared Cherokee boy declared.

"It was a possum, just like I said."

Peering down through the water, Billy was more concerned with his drowned flashlight than the harmless creature on shore.

"Their eyes glow red when you shine a light in them," he added.

"Oh," Chigger replied sheepishly. "I knew that."

The two boys had known each other since the first grade. Most days after school they had played together outdoors. In those days, Chigger's dad worked at a plant nursery near the shores of the lake. On Saturdays he often took the pair with him to work on the plants, trees, and shrubs the nursery grew.

Of course, the boys ended up playing hide-and-seek among the long rows of greenery. And their favorite fishing spot was the inlet of water where they were now. It was near the old nursery that had gone out of business.

Chigger's fishing pole jerked in his hands.

"I think I've got a bite!" he whispered excitedly.

They always whispered when they were fishing. Even though the water muffled human noises, Grandpa Wesley taught Billy that it was best to avoid sudden movements or sharp sounds. Such things could spook the fish.

Chigger yanked the line up out of the water. He found nothing but a water turtle hooked on the end of it.

"Ah, another turtle," Chigger said. "That's the third one tonight! They musta chased off all the fish."

"Have you forgotten that turtles are good luck?" Billy asked as he unhooked the five-pound turtle from his friend's line. "After all," he continued. "It was Grandmother Turtle who brought up the mud from the bottom of the waters so Creator could make land."

He let the turtle slip back into the dark water. It paddled quickly away.

"And that's why we call this land Turtle Island," Chigger said, repeating a phrase he'd heard over and over since he was a kid. "I remember that old Cherokee story just as good as you do."

"One man's myth is another man's religion," Billy replied, using one of the sayings his father often used. "But the Grandma Turtle story is more of a fable. You know, a traditional story that teaches us something."

"Ooh! Did you just go all college professor on me or what?" Chigger laughed.

Billy's father was in fact a college professor who taught Cherokee history and culture at the nearby college. Chigger liked to bring his friend, the professor's son, back down to the grassroots level whenever he started sounding too smart.

"Myth, fable, whatever," Chigger said.

"For someone who doesn't believe in ancient Native folktales, you sure do spook easily."

"Old Indian stories are one thing," Chigger said. "But ghosts and hauntings and glowing red eyes in the night are something different. These eerie activities have been documented on reality TV."

"Ha!" Billy said much louder than he intended to. "Reality TV is just a mindless pastime. But there's something behind old Cherokee legends. Hidden wisdom that's usually true at a deeper level."

"Enough, Professor. You're making my head hurt."

Billy knew he'd pushed it too far.

"Let's call it a night," he said.

"Might as well," Chigger agreed. "Ain't nothin' bitin' but terrapins."

Chigger untied the rope and pulled the lantern up into the boat. They were in a fifteen-foot skiff with a flat bottom. The boat's flat bottom let them get in and out of shallow, reedy water where fish liked to hide.

Though the fishing boat had a motor, Billy didn't like to disturb the silence of nature on nights like this one. Another habit he'd learned from his grandpa. He and Chigger used a pair of oars to propel the vessel toward the shore.

"What could be better than this?" Billy asked, as they glided along the surface of the lake. High above them was a dark, velvet sky filled with twinkling stars.

"A bowl of homemade ice cream would taste pretty good right about now," Chigger replied.

"No, seriously," Billy said, giving his friend a sharp look. "Two full-blood Cherokees on a summer night surrounded by the wonders of nature." He looked up at the sky. "What could be better?"

"Nothing," Chigger had to admit, as he gazed upward as well. "Absolutely nothing."

The only sounds that night were about a thousand chirping bullfrogs, a million clacking cicadas, and the splashing of two oars lightly stroking the water.

The boys soon arrived at the concrete boat launch. Chigger held the boat steady while Billy walked up the slight hill to fetch his pickup truck and boat trailer.

Moments later he backed the trailer down the ramp and into the shallow water. Chigger guided the boat onto the trailer, and then he cranked the trailer's winch to secure it in place. With the boat firmly tied down, the pair headed for home.

Billy knew the Oklahoma back roads of the Cherokee Nation like he knew the back of his own hand. Every twist, turn, pothole, and crack was etched into his mind.

Almost every day of his life, he and Grandpa Wesley had driven those roads and hiked the nearby trails in search of wildlife and wonder. Each trip had included the telling of an old Cherokee legend. The legends recounted ancient tribal teachings in the ways of Native medicine.

While other kids grew up hearing stories of Goldilocks or Little Red Riding Hood, Billy heard about the customs of his people. His grandpa was like a walking, talking library of Native knowledge and outdoor lore.

Fifteen minutes after leaving the lake, they reached Chigger's family's mobile home. It was up a rough dirt road just east of the capital of the Cherokee Nation.

"Did you register for the blowgun contest at this year's Cherokee Holiday?" Chigger asked before getting out of Billy's truck.

"And the cornstalk bow-and-arrow shoot," Billy confirmed. "What about you?"

"Yep," Chigger replied. "Just like last year. Only difference is, I'm gonna beat you at both of 'em this year."

He slammed the truck door and ran toward his mobile home before Billy could respond.

"You're on!" Billy shouted loud enough for his friend to hear. Then Billy sped off into the night. In another twenty minutes, Billy reached his own home near Park Hill, south of Chigger's house.

He pulled into the tree-lined driveway that led to his two-story log home. Parking beside the driveway in his usual graveled spot, he opened the truck's glove box. He took out the pocket watch he kept there. It had belonged to his great-grandfather, Jim "Bullseye" Buckhorn. His grandfather was a famous bow-and-arrow hunter in his day.

The watch's antique hands pointed straight up. Midnight. Later than he said he'd be home. Giving the watch stem a couple of winds, he put the watch back in the glove box. And as he slipped out of his truck, he looked up at the log house.

The lights were still on in his father's upstairs library study. Billy knew that he was busy preparing for the classes he taught at the college.

Stepping quietly onto the porch, he took off his muddy wet boots and left them outside. He tried to keep from making any noise as he moved into the front of the house. He didn't notice the dark shadow of someone sitting on the couch.

"Home kinda late, aren't you?" a woman's voice said from the darkness. Billy nearly jumped out of his skin.

"Ma, you startled me," he replied, trying to catch his breath. "Why are you sitting in the dark?"

"Just collecting my thoughts," she said, turning on a nearby table lamp. She was still in her white nurse's uniform she wore during her nightly shift at the hospital. The whiteness of her uniform contrasted with her black hair and bronze Cherokee skin.

"I know you still think it's summer, young man," she said in a calm tone. "But classes have been going on for a week now. I received a message from your school today. It said you haven't quite been attending on a regular basis."

"Ma, you know I can never get serious about classes until after Labor Day weekend," Billy protested. "That's when summer is really over. It's not fair that they robbed us of the last two weeks of summer."

"It's too bad you inherited your stubborn streak from my side of the family. Your tendency to rebel against authority is from your father's," his mother commented.

"And they never cover anything important in the first few days anyway," Billy added to his defense.

"I'll put this to you as directly as I can," she said, ignoring his protest and standing up. "I expect you to be in class all day every day this coming week. If you miss even one class, then you won't be able to take part in any of the activities you've planned during the following Labor Day weekend. No bow-and-arrow shoot, no blowgun competition, no all-night stomp dance, and no fishing contest."

"But Chigger's counting on me to—"

"You should've thought of all that before you skipped class."

"But—"

"But nothing!" his mother said firmly. "Now go to your room and get in bed. And tomorrow you'll stay home until you've written your summer reading report!"

"Aw, not that," Billy moaned.

"You have read the book, haven't you?"

"Not exactly."

"Of course you haven't," she said, almost in despair. "All the more reason for you to stay home."

She walked toward Billy with her hand out.

"Give me your truck keys," she demanded.

"What?"

"You heard me. Stubborn and rebellious. So put the truck keys in my hand right now!"

He pulled the keys out of his pocket and dropped them into her outstretched hand. One of the things Billy loved about his parents was the freedom they'd always allowed him. It had given him a sense of confidence and freedom at an early age. But he figured he'd pushed it just a little too far this time.

"You can have them back after you've finished the report," she said as she headed for the stairs. "If it's not done by Monday morning, your father or I will take you to school."

His mother marched up the stairs, twirling his set of keys around her index finger.

Billy's shoulders slumped. His head drooped. He trudged toward his room in the back of the house. His summer had come crashing to an end.

CHAPTER 2
A Good Day

The tribe had been putting on the annual Cherokee National Holiday during Labor Day weekend for at least sixty years. It included a lot of old-time Cherokee activities, such as the cornstalk bow-and-arrow shooting contest and the blowgun contest that Billy liked so much. Most of these events took place at the Cherokee Nation cultural grounds located near the tribal offices.

But there were dozens and dozens of other Native cultural events, displays, and activities that brought thousands of Cherokees from all over the United States back home at that time. On top of all that, there were also plenty of other events to occupy a person's time, such as a classic car show, softball tournament, bingo, and a powwow.

But Billy preferred to focus on four specific activities during that weekend. These activities he learned from his Grandpa Wesley. Only two of them were official events of the holiday: the cornstalk shoot and the blowgun contest. The other two, the stomp dance and the fishing contest, took place at other spots away from the Cherokee headquarters.

Taking part in these events was the highlight of Billy's year. That's why it had been important for him to obey his mother's orders completely the days before the big weekend.

He finished the summer reading project and wrote the report in one day. Then he made sure to arrive at school on time every day and stay until the final bell rang. On Friday he'd even asked the school secretary to call his mother and tell her he'd attended class all week.

However, there was one more event Billy had to survive before he could enjoy the coming activities. Every year on the Friday evening before the holiday weekend, both sides of his family gathered for dinner at his house. And that could be a very tense time indeed. Actually, it could be like World War III.

Billy's father, James T. Buckhorn, had come from a long line of Cherokee people who had resisted taking up the white man's ways for many years. But early in life he'd chosen teaching as his path.

Billy's mother, whose maiden name was Rebecca Sarah Ross, came from a family of Cherokee country preachers. They had long ago adopted many of the white man's ways, including religion, partly as a way to survive. Rebecca's brother, John Ross, was, of course, Billy's uncle. He was a well-known preacher in Native church circles.

From direct experience, Billy knew that when these two families got together, an unholy war of words was possible. His own mother and father, both more accepting in their views, acted as buffers between the two extremes of his family.

Thankfully, Grandpa Wesley had been able to come to this year's dinner. He had fallen recently, hurt his knee, and hadn't been as active as he used to be. Now he walked with a cane.

"Our Heavenly Father, we pray for the sinners among us tonight," Uncle John began the prayer before supper. "May they see the light before it's too late."

"And may both sides of this family come together for the sake of our children," Billy's mother suddenly added. "Amen." She ended the prayer much sooner than her preacher brother had intended. He could pray for hours.

"Now let's all enjoy the food that the mothers, aunts, and sisters of these families have prepared for us," Billy's father added. "And may we use it to feed our bodies in a good way so that we may help others."

Billy followed his grandpa as they filled their plates with large portions from the buffet spread across a long table. Billy didn't notice the approach of his uncle.

"Billy, I understand you've begun high school this year," John said in a booming preacher's voice that almost caused Billy to drop his plate.

"Yes, Uncle, I'm in tenth grade." The boy put down his plate for a moment so he could shake the man's hand. Being polite to his elders was something he'd been taught from a very young age.

Grandpa Wesley continued to move on down the buffet line. He left Billy alone to speak to his uncle.

"I certainly hope you won't be taking part in that devil dance out at the Live Oak stomp grounds this year. Nothing good can come of it."

Having overheard this comment, Wesley stepped back to Billy's side.

"Actually, he and I will be dancing briskly all night Saturday," the old man said, loud enough to be heard all around. "Renewing our pledge to the old ways will bring good fortune and health to the entire family."

Moving quickly, Billy's mother appeared beside her preacher brother and said, "Could I speak to you for a minute outside?" John nodded, followed her through the sliding glass door, and stepped out to the back porch.

Billy couldn't hear their words, but he knew what they were saying. It was a quarrel they'd had for years. His mom would say that she'd raised her son to make up his own mind about cultural and spiritual matters. And her brother would argue that his nephew would not make it to heaven if he didn't put aside those old Indian beliefs and come to church. On and on it went.

Meanwhile, Billy's dad came to his side, and they both watched the quarrel unfold through the glass door.

"One man's myth is another man's religion," they said simultaneously and laughed.

"Come out on the front porch with me for a moment," his dad said. They went out to the front of the house for a father-son talk.

"Your mother and I are pleased that you focused on your school duties this past week,"

Mr. Buckhorn told his son. "Your classroom education is every bit as important as the cultural education you get from Grandpa."

He reached into his pocket and pulled out two twenty-dollar bills.

"As a reward, here's a little spending money for you to use this weekend," he said with a smile. Billy took the cash, put it in his back pocket, and then hugged his father.

"We'll be there for the blowgun match tomorrow afternoon," his father said, and added, "Good luck," before going back inside.

And so the holiday weekend had begun with only a minor skirmish between the Buckhorns and the Rosses. Billy was definitely ready for better things to come.

The next morning, Billy met Chigger early for the bow-and-arrow shooting contest.

"Where's your grandpa?" Chigger asked. "He usually comes to see you shoot."

"He's taking care of his hurt knee today," Billy replied. "He soaks it in a tub of herbal medicine and drinks a nasty-tasting tea. Straight out of the Cherokee medicine book."

"Why doesn't he just go to the Indian clinic and get medicine?" Chigger asked. "After all, your mother is a nurse."

"You know he doesn't believe in white man's medicine," Billy answered. "Only for emergencies—serious emergencies."

"Oh, right," Chigger said.

"And he wants to be rested and ready for tonight's stomp dance," Billy added.

"You two haven't missed that for years, have you?" Chigger asked.

"No, we haven't," Billy said. "It's part of the old Cherokee religion that Grandpa insists we do. He says Grandma usually visits him during this ceremony."

Billy's grandmother, Awinita, passed away ten years earlier. Her name means "baby deer" in Cherokee. Billy barely remembered her because he was only six when she died. Grandpa said he continued to see her spirit from time to time. He would see her wandering through the old house they'd shared or hanging around the small garden in back of their house.

Grandpa also said he always saw her during the Labor Day weekend stomp dance. Billy had never seen her, though many people at the stomp dance claimed to have seen loved ones who'd passed away. It was one of the reasons that some people still danced the old dance.

Billy and Chigger had a good day of friendly rivalry. The bow-and-arrow shoot only allowed the use of handmade bows and arrows, so it reinforced that part of Cherokee culture.

The same was true for the blowgun contest. Only handmade blowguns, made of ten- to twelve-foot river cane, could be used. Not very many people could still craft these weapons or the six-inch darts that served as ammunition.

The two friends had hunted, fished, and camped together for the past five years or so. It is how they got to learn and practice these skills. Sometimes Billy's father and grandfather had taken the boys for a weekend adventure. Other times it had been Chigger's dad or uncle who had gone with them.

But in the last couple of years, it had been just the two boys taking these outings. Their parents and relatives had gotten too busy or too old. And the teens were feeling more like they wanted to do things on their own.

But the stomp dance was an activity Billy only did with his grandfather. Besides, Chigger's family wasn't into the "old Indian religion."

The day's contests ended with Billy and Chigger sharing the third-place prize in the bow-and-arrow event, which gave them each fifty bucks and a trophy to share. The trophy, it was decided, would live at Billy's house half the year and Chigger's house the other half.

But in the blowgun contest, nobody could beat or even match Billy Buckhorn. He took first place, ahead of Cherokee men of every age. He got to keep that hundred-dollar prize and trophy all to himself.

Chigger came in fourth place, just out of the prize money. Again. He was almost sure that Billy had some secret skill he'd learned from this grandpa that made him so good at the blowgun. Like a sixth sense or something.

"Someday you'll have to tell me your winning blowgun secret," Chigger said.

"Someday I will," Billy said with a smile. "Someday."

"It's a good thing we're on the same team for Monday's fishing tournament," Chigger said as the boys parted ways at the end of the day.

"Good thing," Billy echoed.

CHAPTER 3
Flash, Crash, Boom

Grandpa picked up Billy at around seven o'clock that night. They headed toward the Live Oak Ceremonial Dance Grounds several miles south of town. All of the Cherokee stomp dance grounds were hidden away from outsiders. No billboards or directional signs pointed the way. Only those who belonged within the circle attended.

The Cherokee stomp dance was a very old ceremony practiced by Billy's people for centuries. The sacred fire was at the center of the event. It was built within an outdoor fireplace constructed of large logs pointed in the four directions. Each of the seven original Cherokee grounds was known for something special. Live Oak, one of only two grounds still in use, is known for putting people in touch with their ancestors.

The singers and dancers circled that fire all night, singing songs that honor elements of nature and the spirit force behind all of creation. The seven Cherokee clans are represented within the ceremonial grounds by seven brush arbors that are placed outside the circle of dancers.

Grandpa Wesley and Billy arrived before the dancing began. As a known medicine man of the Red Paint Clan, Wesley took his seat in his clan's arbor. Since the age of thirteen, Billy had joined his Grandpa in that arbor and was accepted as a member of the same clan. He took a seat next to his grandpa in that arbor.

Clan membership was usually determined by what clan your mother belonged to. Billy should have been a member of the Wolf Clan because his mother was of that clan. And the mother's brothers were usually in charge of teaching a boy the Cherokee ways. But Billy's mother's brothers were Baptist church leaders and not involved in the old-style ceremonies. So Wesley took over Billy's lessons in tribal traditions.

When the night sky had become good and dark, the call for the first round of dancing went out all over the camp. Unlike a powwow, where a drum group provides both the singing and the beat, a stomp dance's rhythm comes from the turtle-shell rattles worn by the women dancers. Rows of these rattles, tied to pieces of leather about the size of a cowboy boot, are strapped to each of a woman's legs just above the ankle. Small pebbles within the shells create a rattle sound with each step a dancer takes.

Billy fell into line behind the circle of dancers as they moved around the center fire. The song leader at the head of the circle sang out the song's first line. The dancers who followed repeated his words like an echo. Thus began the pattern that would last all night.

After a few songs, Wesley joined the dancers, in spite of his bad knee. Throughout the night, singers and dancers drink an herbal tea prepared by stomp dance leaders. That mixture includes natural medicines that keep muscles from cramping while also helping the dancers to stay awake.

After midnight, the ancestor spirits began arriving. They'd been called from their resting place in the Land of the Dead to the west. Though not visible to everyone, some of those spirits took their places in the line of dancers. Others found room in the arbors, each according to his or her clan. Thus the spirits of the living and the spirits of the dead were connected.

By about two o'clock in the morning, Billy was feeling strange. He took a seat in the Red Paint Clan arbor and closed his eyes. Soon he entered the trance-like state of mind that is part of the ceremony. This is when it's possible to have a vision or receive messages from ancestor spirits. Each person's experience, if he has such an experience, is his own.

It wasn't long before an image appeared in Billy's mind. He was on a ladder that led into a low set of glowing clouds just above him. He counted a total of thirteen rungs on the ladder, and he stood on the third rung from the bottom.

As he looked at the ladder, the fourth rung began to glow. It seemed to be inviting him to step up to it. As he began to take that step, the ladder shook. The movement caused him to miss the next rung, and he fell. He woke up from the vision as he hit the ground next to the seat he'd been sitting in.

At about the same time, but unknown to Billy, Wesley was having a vision of his own. The spirit of his beloved wife, Awinita, appeared to be standing in the middle of the fire. That was the vision he hoped he would see, and she appeared only to him. She reached her arms out toward Wesley and spoke to him in his mind.

He heard, "An evil has come into the Cherokee Nation. An evil that must be defeated and removed. You are much too old and crippled to face this, Wesley. Therefore, Billy must be called on sooner than expected. But he will need your help to take the step before him so that he may, in turn, help the Nation."

Then, with great energy, she sent a wave of love directly into her husband's heart. The power of that wave caused the old man to pass out. He fell to the ground a few feet from the fire. Several nearby dancers turned, picked him up, and carried him back to his arbor.

Billy was just coming out of his trance as they brought his grandfather in and laid him on a bench. One of the men told Billy what had happened. One of the women placed a rolled-up towel under Wesley's head to make him more comfortable.

Billy knelt beside his elder and replayed the ladder vision in his mind so he wouldn't forget it. Wesley began to stir. He opened his eyes and found Billy at his side.

"Your grandma put in an appearance," he said with a smile. "And she gave me a message about you and the future of the Cherokees."

Billy did not expect to be part of his grandma's message.

"I had a vision as well," he said.

Each told the other of his vision. Each sat in wonder at what they'd experienced.

"What does it all mean?" Billy asked.

"Only time will tell," Wesley replied. "Nature will give us a sign over the next few days that will confirm these messages. We'll just have to wait and watch. Now, to give thanks to the spirits for what has been revealed to us, we must go back to the fire and resume dancing."

"Where's your cane, Grandpa?" Billy asked as he helped the elder to his feet.

"It's leaning over there in the corner. But I won't need it until morning when the ceremony is over."

With that, the pair joined in the next round of dances. Billy's mind raced with questions, but he knew that only patience and time would reveal the answers. He and his grandpa danced until dawn.

Luckily, Sunday had been planned as a day off for Billy. He needed the day to rest after the all-night dance. And that's what he did most of the day—rest.

Monday was fishing-contest day. At the crack of dawn, Billy was up and had his skiff hitched to his pickup. His fishing gear was already loaded in the boat. Chigger arrived around 6:30 a.m. with his fishing gear.

"I made some biscuits and gravy for you boys," Billy's mother said, as she came out of the house carrying a paper sack. "You need to eat a hearty breakfast to keep up your strength today."

"Thanks, Ma," Billy replied, taking the sack and giving her a little peck on the cheek. "Chigger also brought some dried deer jerky, so we won't go hungry."

She almost told them to be careful, as they jumped in the truck to leave. She held her tongue though, knowing that sixteen-year-old boys don't want to hear a mother's concerns. But Mrs. Buckhorn was definitely feeling some sense of worry as she watched the pair head out. *What was that about?* she wondered. But she had no clue.

About two dozen Cherokee fishermen registered for the contest that morning on the shores of the lake. Cash prizes would be given for the most fish caught, the largest fish caught, and the smallest fish caught. That last category was included to get younger fishermen to compete.

Billy and Grandpa had won a little prize money before for either the largest fish or most fish caught. This was Billy's first year to go it without his grandfather, and he kind of missed seeing the old man that morning. At the same time, he felt okay about fishing the contest with Chigger.

The contest would end at 6:00 p.m. Anyone who hadn't returned to the main dock by that time would be excluded. Promptly at 8:00 a.m. the contest began. Boats sped off in every direction as each team of anglers headed for their favorite spots.

Billy and Chigger headed west toward an inlet that on a map looked like the mouth of a wolf's head in profile. He couldn't figure out why no one had named it Wolf's Head Inlet or Wolf's Mouth Bay. It was a place where he and Wesley had caught many a fish.

As soon as they hit the inlet, they began working the shallow, reedy shoreline with a cane pole. The pair moved along parallel to the land for an hour, only getting an occasional nibble. *We have to change tactics,* Billy thought. *And maybe bait, too.*

Switching to rods and reels, the boys tried casting spinner lures just beyond the edge of the reeds. That's what those largemouth bass were looking for. These spinners were made of shiny metal pieces that twisted and turned as they moved through the water.

Billy and Chigger began getting strikes about every other cast. By late morning they had a dozen bass of various sizes.

As the sun climbed in the sky, the boys moved into deeper water. They knew that as the water heated up, some of the larger fish would move into deeper, cooler water. They put something called stink bait on their hooks and dropped their lines down about forty feet. That's where the catfish would be hanging out, near the bottom of the lake.

Billy liked the way the day's fishing was going. He and Chigger were pulling in almost as many fish as he and Grandpa had caught together last year.

Wouldn't Wesley be surprised, he thought.

That's when they heard the first distant thunder. They looked to the west, the direction the rumble had come from. Large thunder clouds were gathering and building. This was a common sight in eastern Oklahoma this time of year.

"Those tall, flat-bottomed clouds always look like stacks of cotton balls sitting on top of dinner plates," Billy told Chigger, who laughed at the idea.

Billy checked his pocket watch and saw that it was almost 3:00 p.m. Looking up at the clouds again, he noticed they were moving rapidly toward them. Just then a flash of lightning jumped from cloud to cloud.

"Guess we'd better start moving toward the shore," Billy advised. "And get off the water."

"I'll drive," Chigger suggested. "You can fish as we go."

Billy nodded his okay. Before heading toward the shore, the guys put on their lightweight rain ponchos. Then Billy released a little bit of line from his reel and let it trail behind the boat. Chigger started the motor and set it to a slow speed. The shiny spinner lure followed behind the boat as it slowly crept through the water.

Quickly, the wind came up just as a sheet of rain pushed across the water. It seemed as though thunderclouds had appeared overhead out of nowhere. Then a flash of lightning burst across the sky overhead, followed immediately by crash of thunder. A loud crash. The storm was already on top of them.

"We'd better get off the water now," Chigger said. "Pull your line in."

Billy began reeling in his spinning lure.

Chigger looked across the lake to locate the nearest shoreline. There was a rocky finger of land that jutted out into the water. He saw other anglers already landing their boats in that area. He had to turn their skiff directly into the wind to reach that point.

He'd just made the turn when Billy stood up in the front of the boat. He was trying to keep the fishing line away from the boat's motor.

Chigger was about to tell his friend to sit down and hold on because he was going to give the boat motor full throttle. But he never got a chance to say or do anything else.

All at once a bright flash of light engulfed the boys. At the same time, a deafening BOOM washed over them. A single bolt of electricity hit the water near the front of the boat. It raced along the surface of the water and into Billy's metal spinner as he pulled it up out of the water. Then the electric pulse jumped from the spinner to Billy's rod and into the boy's body.

The electric shock ran through Billy's flesh and bones and up into his brain. At that moment, the world around him seemed to switch from positive to negative. Colors reversed themselves. Time shifted into slow motion. Billy had never felt anything like it. Then he blacked out.

The jolt lifted Billy up and threw him backward in the skiff. He landed right on top of Chigger sitting in the back. The force knocked Chigger out cold.

When he woke up, Chigger was in the back of an ambulance. He moaned and looked around. He saw two emergency medical attendants working on Billy, who was laying on a gurney.

"What . . . what happened?" Chigger struggled to ask.

"You'll be all right," one of the attendants said. "I can't say the same for your friend here. He took a direct hit, and he's lucky to be alive. But we've got to get him to the hospital fast."

CHAPTER 4
The Aftershock

While in the ambulance, Billy went in and out of consciousness. At one point it felt like his whole body was on fire. At another point it seemed like every muscle had drawn up and clenched tightly. So tightly he couldn't relax them. And there was that smell. The smell of burning flesh.

After that, Billy slipped into a temporary coma. A strange array of images floated through his mind while he was unconscious. Memories from his childhood, bits of stories his grandpa had told him, a fleeting glimpse of his grandma Awinita, and the ladder he'd seen at the stomp dance. All these drifted past him as he floated in darkness.

Billy awoke from the coma a couple of days later. His mom and dad were both there in his hospital room. Someone else seemed to be in the room too. But that someone stayed just out of view. It was more like Billy felt his presence rather than saw him. It was certainly a him, though.

"Oh, Billy, you had us so worried," his mother said. She was wearing her nurse's uniform. "I'm so glad I was on duty when they brought you in." She checked the screen on one of the machines that stood near Billy's bed.

"Glad to see you're back, son," his father said, as he approached from the other side of the bed. "We've kept watch over you twenty-four hours a day for two days."

"Where's Grandpa?" Billy asked.

"Your grandpa was here earlier, but we sent him home to get some rest," his mother replied. "He said to call him when you woke up."

Billy's mouth was dry and he began smacking his lips. Noticing that her son was thirsty, Mrs. Buckhorn grabbed the glass of water sitting on a tray table beside the bed.

She held the glass close to him, and he sipped water through the straw. As he drank, he realized he didn't even know why he was in the hospital.

"What happened?" he asked after swallowing a big sip. "I don't remember."

"A group of people standing on the shore saw you get hit by a bolt of lightning," his dad reported. "They jumped in their boat and sped out to get you and Chigger."

"One of them called here to the hospital, and we sent out an ambulance," his mother added.

"Chigger. What about Chigger?" Billy was more awake now.

"He's just fine," Billy's father answered. "The lightning didn't hit him, but he's at home taking it easy for a couple of days."

Then Billy's mother gave his dad a funny look. He nodded to her.

"Billy, there's something I need to prepare you for," his mother said. "You have burn patterns in a couple of places left there by the lightning."

"Burn patterns?" the boy asked. "What kind of burn patterns?"

His mother opened a nearby cabinet and pulled out a hand mirror. She returned to the bed and pulled back the sheet that covered Billy's right hand. For the first time he saw that a bandage covered the back of his hand.

Then she held up the mirror for him to see that there was a larger, similar bandage on the side of his neck. He reached up and touched the neck bandage.

"Why don't I feel any pain here?" he asked.

"We've covered both places with numbing medicine," his mother, the nurse, answered. "When the doctor comes in to check on you, he'll let you see the burns."

"Okay," Billy said, gently rubbing the bandage on his hand.

"Now that I know you're all right, I have to get back to the college," his dad said. "A substitute has been filling in for me. I'll check in on you this evening."

As his father left the room, Billy's doctor stepped in and moved toward the bed. He was an Anglo man in his fifties, wearing a white coat and dark-rimmed glasses.

"I'm Dr. Jackson," the man said, extending his hand. Billy reached out to shake the doctor's hand. The doctor shook it gently and then turned it sideways to look at the bandage.

"Did your mother tell you about the burn marks?"

"She said there was some kind of pattern," Billy replied. "Can I see it?"

"Sure," the doctor answered. He carefully pulled back one side of the gauze on the back of Billy's hand to reveal a red pattern that looked a little like a spider web. Jagged red lines, like bicycle spokes, radiated out from a dark red spot in the center. Two sets of finer red lines connected all the spokes.

As Billy stared at the markings on his hand, Dr. Jackson pulled back the bandage on the side of his patient's neck. Billy's mother handed the mirror to the doctor, and he held it up for Billy to see. A larger version of the web-like pattern spread across his neck.

"Oh my god!" Billy blurted. "I look like a freak."

"Young man, you're lucky to be alive," the doctor said. "And until the burns heal, we won't know how visible the scars will be."

"Scars?" Billy's mother said with motherly concern. "There will be scars?"

"I'm afraid so," the doctor confirmed. He turned to Billy's mom. "Nurse, I think it's time for your son to eat something and get some rest. Would you mind calling down to the kitchen and asking them to send up a tray of food?"

"Sure thing, doctor," Billy's mother replied. She stepped out to go to the nurse's station to order some food.

"How bad do you think the scarring will be?" Billy asked Dr. Jackson after his mother had gone.

"As I said, you're lucky to be alive. And you'll always have these markings as a reminder of that. I wouldn't worry too much about the scars."

The doctor checked Billy's medical chart, which hung from a clip on the end of his bed.

"All your vital signs look good," he said, returning the chart to its place. He then stepped back to the side of Billy's bed and said reassuringly, "Looks like you're healing just fine. I'll check in on you later."

He left, and Billy was alone in the room. Well, almost alone. He could still "feel" that someone else was around.

"Who's there?" he called out.

There was no answer.

"I know you're in here. I can't see you, but I can feel you."

"If I show myself, will you promise not to freak out?" the small voice of a man asked.

"If you don't show yourself, I'll call the nurse in here to chase you out," Billy answered. "I'm going to count to three. One. Two."

"Just like when you were a little kid," the voice said, as a small Native American man stepped out from under Billy's bed.

The man was only about two feet tall and had a long braid of black hair. He wore a pair of fringed leather pants and moccasins. A look of shock spread across Billy's face at the sight of him.

"Remember?" the little man asked. "Your mother would count to three before making you go to bed at night or eat your vegetables."

"You're not real," Billy stated firmly. "My father said there was no such thing as Little People. That was just an ancient myth—a way to explain odd things. The Irish have leprechauns and the Cherokee have Little People."

"That's not what you told Chigger the other day," the little man replied. "What happened to the idea that there was a deeper truth beneath the legends?"

"How do you know about that?"

"I know a lot about you, and it hurts me deeply that you don't remember me," the little man said. "You don't remember the times we spent exploring the woods behind your house when you were five years old?"

When he said that, a mental image flashed in Billy's mind. He was out in the woods behind the old frame house where he used to live. A game of hide-and-seek was under way. Billy was hiding in a big pile of fallen leaves. A voice called out.

"Come out, come out, wherever you are!"

As the mental movie played on, the leaves parted and the five-year-old Billy was looking out at a face. The face of the little Indian man who now stood in his hospital room.

"Now I remember," the sixteen-year-old Billy blurted out. "Little Wolf, is it really you?"

"Bingo, Billy!" the little man said excitedly. "You remembered!"

"But I thought I had imagined you," Billy said with confusion in his voice.

"It happens all the time," Little Wolf said. "Kids grow up, lose interest, and forget about their childhood pals. It's because, as you get older, you spend less and less time in your mind and more and more time in the outside world."

"Then why am I seeing you now?"

"Things have changed," Little Wolf replied. "You have changed."

"Because of the lightning?"

"Because of the lightning," Little Wolf confirmed. "And because of who you are becoming."

"What do you mean by that?"

Just then the door to Billy's hospital room opened. Billy looked up to see his mother bringing in a tray of food. He looked back down to where Little Wolf had been standing. The little man was gone.

"Who are you talking to?" Billy's mother asked as she set the tray down.

"Ah, no one," Billy said. "I'm in here alone."

"Oh, I thought I heard you talking to someone," she said. "Here's your lunch. Are you okay?"

"Yeah, sure," Billy said. "Why wouldn't I be?"

"People have some strange experiences after being hit by lightning," she said, checking the monitor beside the bed. "It takes the brain awhile to fully recover from the electric shock. People have reported weird visions and odd dreams. But they should clear up in a week or so."

"That's good to know," Billy said, not willing to admit his own experience. "I'll let you know if anything like that comes up."

"Good," his mother replied. "I'll bring you some magazines and check in on you later," she said. "Now eat your lunch and get some rest."

After she left, Billy looked around the room. He leaned over far enough to check under his bed. No sign of Little Wolf.

Billy was starting to remember other things about his childhood friend. One thing was that no one but Billy could see him. He and Billy would be playing together outside. Then one of Billy's parents would come find him. But they could never see Little Wolf, even though the little Indian might be standing right next to him.

Of course, now that Billy thought of it, they were always outside. Never inside. And there had been a couple of times when Little Wolf had said they should go somewhere else to play. One time they moved to the other side of the house just before a dead tree fell right where they'd been playing. Billy would've been crushed.

Another time Little Wolf said Billy should go inside. A few minutes later, a mountain lion was seen prowling in their backyard. That had to be more than chance. Could an imaginary friend do those things? The answer to that question would have to wait. Memories of the little man made Billy sleepy. Soon he was fast asleep in the middle of the afternoon.

CHAPTER 5
The Bird Man

Billy was released from the hospital a few days later. He told no one about the return of Little Wolf, at first hoping it was one of the after effects of the lightning his mother had spoken about. Yet almost everywhere Billy went, he thought he saw the little Indian lurking in a corner or peering out from behind a bush.

The main outward reminders of Billy's encounter with lightning were the scars that had formed on the back of his hand and the side of his neck. The web-like pattern had not faded. Dr. Jackson had explained that the center points were the places where the electricity had entered Billy's body. If you didn't know better, you'd think they were tattoos with ragged edges. They gave him a kind of eerie look.

When Grandpa Wesley saw the web-like scars on his grandson, he said, "What could be more perfect?"

"What's so perfect about them?" Billy asked. "I look like I belong in a freak show."

"Have you forgotten that it was Water Spider who brought Fire to the Cherokee people?" Grandpa asked.

Grandpa must have told him a hundred times the story of how Fire came to humans. In the beginning of the world, the only ones who had Fire were the Thunders, who lived up beyond the sky. One day they sent Lightning down to a tree in the center of an island, and that's where Fire began on earth. All the animals wanted to go get Fire and bring it to the mainland for everyone to use. Many animals tried and failed. It was the lowly Water Spider who cleverly devised a way to bring Fire across the water for all to use.

"So the Thunders sent Fire again to the Cherokee people through you," Grandpa said. "It's a clear sign that the spirits are ready for you to take the next steps on your medicine journey. And a sign that you'll be aided by supernatural powers on that journey."

This left Billy speechless.

"Why me?" he eventually asked. "I'm nobody special."

"Who knows?" Grandpa responded. "Maybe you are."

While Billy was home recovering, his grandfather wasn't his only visitor. He was, of course, thrilled to see Chigger, who came by each day after school.

Less thrilling was the visit Uncle John paid him. Billy's mother escorted her brother into Billy's bedroom, then she went back to the kitchen to make the man some iced tea. When Uncle John was sure his sister was out of hearing range, he spoke in a loud whisper.

"I warned you not to go to that stomp dance, didn't I?" the preacher said. "Well, this is God's punishment on you, boy."

Billy remained silent. The man took Billy's hand in his and pointed to the scars.

"And now you have the mark of the beast for all to see!" His voice was no longer a whisper. He put a hand on Billy's head.

"Get down on your knees and beg for forgiveness!" he shouted loud enough for Billy's mother to hear. She rushed to Billy's room.

"All right, that's it," she said angrily to her brother. "It's time for you to leave."

"I'm only trying to save this house from the wrath of the Almighty," John Ross protested. "Repent and ye shall be saved!"

"Leave or I'll call the police," Billy's mother said.

Her brother looked at her in disbelief. "You have sealed your own fate," he said and left.

"I'm so sorry for that," Billy's mother said as she sat on his bed. She hugged her son. "He's gone too far and won't be invited back."

"Thanks, Mother," Billy said. "I'm exhausted." She left the room so her son could rest.

A week after the lightning strike, the doctor said Billy could go back to school. His first day back was kind of weird. Students gathered in groups in the hallways, whispering and staring whenever he walked by. Some teachers did the same thing. You might've thought he just landed from outer space.

The school's Cherokee principal, Mr. Sixkiller, noticed how disruptive this behavior was and decided to quiet everyone down so they could get on with the business of learning.

"You have no doubt noticed that Billy Buckhorn is back in school after his horrific accident," he said during morning notices heard on speakers all over the school. "He is lucky to be alive, and we're lucky to have him back. So I want everyone here at Tahlequah High School to make him feel welcome back in our community."

That helped a little. Not so many students stood around gawking as he walked by. A few actually greeted him and shook his hand. That's when they got close enough to see the burn scars and backed away.

That's just great, Billy thought. *Now I'm a social outcast.*

At least he and Chigger had gym class together. When they got to the gym that afternoon, they learned that a substitute teacher had taken over the class.

"My name is Mr. Ravenwood," the substitute said as he stood in front of the thirty or so boys in the class. He was a tall, thin white man with longish jet-black hair. Billy thought his slightly hooked nose made him look like a bird.

"Your original gym teacher, Mr. Wildcat, suddenly got sick last week and won't be able to return for several weeks," he continued. "I was happy to fill in on short notice. I did a little coaching with the Eastern Cherokees in North Carolina. So I am familiar with your tribe."

Billy took an instant disliking to the man. He didn't know why, but something about the guy bothered him.

"Did you get a weird vibe from the new gym teacher?" Billy asked Chigger after class.

"Not really," his friend answered. "He just kinda looks like a stork or something."

Having missed a week of school, Billy had quite of bit of reading and homework to do to get caught up. So he didn't have time for much else during the next few days. By the middle of the week, he felt dazed and overworked. He studied for his first math test until after midnight on Wednesday.

Then he fell asleep sitting at the desk next to his bed. He'd rested his head on his open algebra book. When he woke up the next morning, he had a terrible neck ache. But there was something else he woke up with. He understood everything in the chapter he'd been struggling with. He wasn't sure how that had happened.

That day's math test actually turned out to be easy for him. He was the first one in class to finish it. That had never happened before.

"I didn't realize that high school would be so much harder than middle school," Chigger told Billy later that day. "The homework is killing me. When are we ever going to have time for anything else?"

"What do you think I'm going through?" Billy replied. "I have a whole week's extra work to plow through." He didn't say anything about acing his math test. He was sure it was a fluke.

That night he needed to study for his first history test. He had a theory he wanted to try out, so he did all his other homework first. On purpose, he didn't look at his history lesson. Then, when it was bedtime, he opened his history textbook to the chapter he needed to study. He placed the book on top of his pillow and laid his head down on it. There he slept all night.

He woke up with a clear head and a good feeling about his history lesson. And when it came time for the exam, it was like a repeat of the math test. He cruised through it and finished first.

Wow, he thought. *What's going on here? Whatever it is, I think I like it!*

What he didn't like, though, was what was going on in gym. It seemed that Mr. Ravenwood often gave Billy long, strange looks. It was like he was studying the sixteen-year-old. Then, when he realized that Billy might have noticed the long stare, the teacher quickly looked away. Or was it all just in Billy's mind?

Billy thought too many strange things had been happening since the lightning strike. So it was time to check in with Grandpa to see if he had any idea of what might be going on. He headed to the old man's house that Saturday morning.

As was usual on a Saturday, a group of Indians sat on Wesley's front porch or in their cars parked in front of the house. They were among the hundreds of people who came to get "doctored" by the old medicine man on a regular basis.

Billy worked his way past the people and went inside. He found Wesley out back gathering herbs to help his patients. Down on all fours, the elderly man was pulling up some roots.

"You have to go deeper and deeper into the woods these days to find many of these medicines," Wesley said as Billy stepped into the garden. "All the houses, roads, and buildings disturb the natural order of things."

The elder reached out his arm to Billy. It showed that he wanted Billy's help with standing up. The boy grabbed the wrinkled brown hand and gently but firmly pulled. As his grandpa got up, Billy thought he saw Little Wolf out of the corner of his eye. He was hiding behind a row of sunflowers. But as the boy looked again, the little man was gone.

"It's a busy morning," Wesley said, brushing the dirt from his clothes. "I need an able helper more with each passing day. Can you stay awhile?"

"Sure, Grandpa," Billy said. "But I need to talk to you first."

"Okay. Let me take these herbs to Mr. Hummingbird and tell him how to use them," Wesley said as he headed back toward the house. "Then I'll pour us a cup of coffee and we can talk."

"As long as you have donuts or fry bread to go with it," Billy said with a smile.

While Wesley was gone, Billy poured them each a cup of coffee and found a couple of donuts in a box that he put on plates. After taking the herbs to the front porch, Wesley returned to the kitchen. Then the two sat down for a serious talk.

"Stuff has been going on since the lightning," Billy began. "Stuff I can't explain."

"That's to be expected," Grandpa said after taking a sip of coffee. "You've entered a new phase of your medicine path. But I may not be able to help you with it much now."

"Why's that, Grandpa?"

"I wasn't chosen by the Thunders," he said. "I don't have the Lightning gifts. But tell me what's been going on. I might at least be able to point you in the right direction."

"Do you remember my childhood friend Little Wolf?" Billy asked after taking a bite of donut.

"Sure I do," Grandpa answered. "If you remember, your grandma and I were the only ones who believed he was real."

"He's back," Billy said. "First he appeared to me in my hospital room. Since then he's been showing up in random places. I just saw him now at the edge of your garden."

"The Little People have made themselves visible to you again," Grandpa said. "That's a very good sign. Now I can tell you the rest of that story."

"What?"

"Little Wolf has been one of my medicine helpers since before you were born," Wesley replied. "In fact, he first appeared to your grandma Awinita right out there in that garden when we were doctoring people together. We sent Little Wolf to you for your own safety."

"Really? Why didn't you tell me this before?"

"Sometimes it's best to let these things unfold naturally," Grandpa answered. "Things need to be revealed in their own good time. What other stuff has been happening?"

"I know this will sound weird," Billy said. "but I can sleep on top of my school books. And when I wake up the next morning, I've learned the lesson for that day."

"That's a new one on me," Wesley admitted. "I'll have to look in my old files to see if anything like that was recorded in the pages of the *Tsalagi Nuwodhi Digohweili, The Cherokee Book of Medicine*. That's what the Old Ones called the original pages, handwritten in the Cherokee alphabet. I inherited an unbound copy of the pages from your great-grandfather."

As he listened, Billy took another couple of sips of his coffee and a bite of his donut.

That gave him time to think about what he was going to say next.

"The last thing is something that's going on at school," he began. "There's a substitute teacher who took over gym classes—a white man, Mr. Ravenwood. He just moved here."

"So? There are plenty of non-Indians working at the school."

"I got a bad feeling about him the very first time I saw him," Billy said. "And he looks at me funny. He doesn't really talk to me, but something just doesn't seem right about the man."

He paused and shook his head.

"I must be seeing things. No one else seems to think there's anything wrong."

"Don't do that to yourself," Wesley advised. "Don't dismiss your intuition, your inner feelings about a situation. You must learn to rely on those instincts more and more. They will grow stronger and seem more real."

Wesley paused to think and drink more coffee.

"If something doesn't feel right to you, then we can't ignore it," he added. "Remember your grandma's message to me at the stomp dance? Something evil has come into the Nation from somewhere outside. We have to keep our insight turned on so we'll recognize this evil when we see it. Who knows what form it takes."

"You think that might have something to do with this new teacher?" Billy asked.

"Maybe so, maybe not," Grandpa answered. "We can't rule anything out at this point, so listen to your inner voice. And allow Little Wolf to help you out if he offers."

After a final sip of coffee, he said, "Now we have to get back to work. Please go out and ask Mrs. Deer-In-Water to come in so we can see what's ailing her.

CHAPTER 6
Wide Open

Word of the boy who survived a lightning strike spread like wildfire throughout eastern Oklahoma. Especially after the news story appeared in the local daily newspaper. A photographer had sneaked into Billy's hospital room. He took a photo of the spider-like burn marks on his neck and hand. Billy was asleep at the time and didn't know someone had snapped the photo until it appeared in print.

Other area newspapers ran similar stories in the days and weeks that followed. At the end of September, a long feature story appeared in the monthly tribal newspaper, the *Cherokee Phoenix*. Some people called Billy's survival a miracle. Others, after seeing the scars, called it demonic, as Billy's uncle had.

"Ignore the news stories," Billy's father said. "It's just media hype designed to sell newspapers. People will forget about it in a couple of weeks."

Billy hoped his father was right.

Back in school the following week, Billy started noticing something else strange going on. It happened when he touched people, shook their hand, or patted them on the back. A series of images flashed in his mind. Sometimes the images were in black and white. Other times they were in color. The pictures formed a quick, little movie starring that person. It even happened when a person handed him something. Both of their hands touched the object at the same time and the movie started.

A girl Billy barely knew dropped a book near him. He reached down to pick it up for her. When he handed the book to her, his hand brushed hers by accident. Quickly he saw a black-and-white picture in his head.

She was being slapped across the face by a boy at school. It stunned Billy for a moment.

Later, his English teacher was returning graded papers to students in class. She and Billy both had a hold on his paper for a brief instant. The color image that flashed in his mind showed her arguing with a man, another teacher, in the parking lot.

The images came and went quickly. But the flash of each movie passed through Billy like a mini-jolt of lightning. It caused him to jerk and stop what he was doing.

But in gym class Billy got the biggest mini-jolt of all. Mr. Ravenwood passed out basketball jerseys to the boys in the class. He handed one to Billy without looking at him. Billy took it directly from the man's hand and a black-and-white image flashed in the boy's mind.

The gym teacher was in a darkened room. He stood over a teenage Native girl. She was screaming as Ravenwood gagged her mouth. In a quick flash, Billy saw the teacher's face and he looked just like a bird. A raven.

The image was so abrupt and shocking that it caused Billy to drop the jersey on the floor. Once the item left his hand, the movie stopped running in his mind.

"I hope you can hold on to the ball better than that, Lightning Boy," the teacher said in a gruff tone. "Now pick it up."

The teacher continued to hand out the shirts, but Billy didn't want to pick up the article of clothing. It seemed to be poisoned. Poisoned by the picture in Billy's head.

What's going on, Billy thought. *Am I losing it? Did the electricity scramble my brain?*

Billy finally got up enough courage to tell his parents and his best friend about the strange thing happening to him. Each had a different reaction.

His father said, "That both fascinates and worries me. It reminds me of the strange case of Bearpaw Perkins a hundred years ago. According to papers in the college archives, he was struck by lightning up on Wild Horse Mountain."

"What happened to him?" Billy asked.

"Eyewitnesses claimed he went on to become a famous medicine man. But later he was taken by aliens."

"Right, Dad," Billy said as he went to see what his mother might say.

"It's probably just a medical condition that will eventually go away," she said at first. But after a few moments of thought, she placed her hand on his forehead to see if he had a fever. Then she shined a small flashlight in his eyes to see if his pupils dilated like they should.

"No signs of concussion or brain swelling," she observed. "We could make an appointment with a therapist, if you'd like to talk about what's going on. You know it's always good to have a mental health professional look into visions and such."

So much for guidance from the professor and the nurse. Billy hoped Chigger would be more open to listening and giving him helpful feedback.

"That's the coolest thing I've ever heard," Chigger exclaimed. "With all the publicity you've been getting, you could have your own reality TV show in no time!"

"Chigger, this is serious stuff," Billy scolded. "I don't want a lot of people knowing about this. It makes me sound crazy."

"Sorry," Chigger replied. "I got carried away."

"I'm trying to figure out why some of the images I see are black and white and why some are in color," Billy said with a serious tone. "Maybe the black-and-white images show things that have already happened. The color images might be future events. What do you think?"

"I think WOW," Chigger said. "My best friend can sleep on his books to study for tests. He can see the past and predict the future. Can I be your manager? This is gonna be big!"

"You're getting carried away again," Billy reminded him. "I told you I don't want any attention."

But Billy couldn't possibly imagine the attention he would soon get.

Later that week, he and Chigger were leaving school. They headed for the parking lot. Thirty or so kids had just boarded a school bus parked at the rear of the school. The driver, an elderly Cherokee man, prepared to make his daily trip over winding, hilly back roads.

Out of the corner of his eye, Billy saw Little Wolf scurrying about. First he was in the bushes near the school. Next he peeked out from behind a car. Then the little Indian ducked under the school bus. Billy looked at Chigger to see if his friend had seen the little man. Chigger seemed clueless.

The two boys passed by the back of the bus. Billy put his hand out and touched the back door of the bus. Instantly an image popped into his mind. In a close-up color view, Billy saw liquid dripping from the engine of the bus. Because he'd worked on cars with his dad, Billy knew the fluid was coming from a brake hose.

In the next image, Billy saw the driver lose control of the bus as he crossed an old bridge. The bus, and all the kids inside, toppled off the bridge and into the water below.

Billy pulled his hand away from the bus and dropped his books. He grabbed his friend's shirt sleeve.

"I have to warn the bus driver," Billy said. "I think this bus is going to crash today."

A look of shock spread across Chigger's face and froze there.

"I told you the things happening to me sound crazy. But I can't let thirty kids get hurt if there's even the smallest chance it might be true."

Billy sprang into action just as the driver started the bus. As the bus doors were closing, Billy thrust his arm between them.

"Hold on!" he yelled at the old man. "You can't leave."

The driver opened the doors wide enough for Billy to climb inside.

"I believe this bus is going to crash today," Billy said with excitement. "You've got to get these kids off and put them on another bus."

"Son, I don't know what drugs you've been taking," the driver said. "You need to step out of the bus. Right now."

The driver's voice was firm but controlled. Then he saw the spider web on Billy's neck. "You're that kid who got struck by lightning," he said loudly. "They said your mind might not be right because of it. Now I know for sure."

The old Indian reached for a two-way radio attached to the dashboard. "This is bus number two-fourteen, still on the high school grounds. I need security here, now! I've got a student causing a ruckus."

Realizing that he wasn't achieving anything, Billy retreated down the steps.

"Let's get out of here before we get in trouble," he said. "I'm probably out of my mind, anyway."

Chigger helped him pick up the books he'd dropped at the back of the bus. Then the boys headed for Billy's truck.

"This is exactly what I was afraid of," Billy said as the boys walked quickly across the parking lot. They pulled out of the parking lot just as a security guard was stepping onto the bus. The boys didn't stick around to find out what would happen next.

At home, Billy didn't mention the school bus event to his parents. He hoped the whole thing would be forgotten and ignored. He at least wanted to have time to talk to Grandpa about it.

However, at around seven o'clock that evening, someone knocked on the Buckhorns' front door. Opening it, Billy's father found a policeman and the principal of Billy's school standing on the porch.

"Mr. Sixkiller, what's this about?" Mr. Buckhorn asked. "Is Billy in some kind of trouble?"

The principal reached out and shook hands with Billy's father.

"There's no trouble, Mr. Buckhorn," the school principal replied. "I want you to meet Lieutenant Swimmer." The officer also shook hands with Billy's father. "May we come in?" the principal asked. "We need to talk to your family about what happened today."

Puzzled by this statement, Billy's father invited the two men inside and called the family to the living room. Billy and his mother took seats on the couch. Then the principal began to explain why they were there.

"What happened today was both amazing and troubling," the principal started. "We're here to thank Billy for his actions this afternoon and ask him a few questions. I assume he told you about the school bus."

"Billy has said nothing about any school bus," Mrs. Buckhorn replied. She looked over at her son.

Lieutenant Swimmer told them about Billy's efforts to stop the bus from leaving the school grounds.

"Billy, why didn't you tell us about this?" his father asked sternly.

"Because it sounded too crazy," Billy said. "Even to me."

"Luckily, the security guard inspected the bus, looking for defects," the policeman said. "To see if there was any reason the bus might crash today."

"And what did he find?" Mr. Buckhorn asked.

"He found that the brake line had a leak," Mr. Sixkiller answered.

"Actually, our crime lab found that it had been cut," Lieutenant Swimmer added.

"What?" Billy said, standing up. "You mean I was right?"

"Yes, son, you saved the lives of the bus driver and thirty kids," the principal said.

"What we want to know is how you knew there was something wrong," the policeman said. "Two detectives on the police force think you're the one who cut that line. That you did it just so you could get attention and become a hero. Or that you cut the line but later had a change of heart. Maybe you couldn't go through with it."

"Now, see here," Mr. Buckhorn stood next to his son. "Billy would never do anything like that." He looked at his son. "Would you, Billy?"

"I've been 'seeing' things lately," Billy blurted out. "Ever since the lightning strike. Little movies run in my head that show me something that has happened to someone. Or maybe something that's about to happen to someone."

There was silence in the room. Billy's parents hadn't taken their son's reports of visions seriously. Now, in the presence of a policeman and a principal, they had to. No one knew what to say.

"I haven't told many people about it because it sounds too weird," Billy continued. "Too crazy. You'd probably do the same thing if you were in my shoes."

"No doubt," the principal said.

"So are you here to thank Billy for saving those kids?" Mr. Buckhorn asked. "Or are you here to arrest him for damaging the bus? Which is it?"

The two visitors stood up.

"As I said, we're here to thank your son," Lieutenant Swimmer answered. "I believe he saved those kids and did nothing to ruin the brakes."

Both Mr. Sixkiller and Lieutenant Swimmer shook Billy's hand and gave him a pat on the back. Billy half expected to see the flash of some image with each touch. He was pleased that no movies ran in his mind.

"But that leaves us with the problem of finding out who did it," Lieutenant Swimmer said as the two men turned to leave. "Who would want to harm a busload of school kids? In my opinion, that would have to be some kind of monster."

Billy and his parents escorted the two visitors to the door. Just as the men were about to leave, the policeman said, "The news media have picked up on this story. Our office has been swamped with calls. We want to hold a press conference to answer their questions. What do you think about that?"

"It's a terrible idea," Billy said. "I've already had too much attention focused on me because of the lightning. I don't want any more. I just want to be a normal kid."

"Okay," the officer replied. "We'll try our best to keep reporters away from the incident. Try to keep a lid on it."

None of them knew that the lid on this story was about to blow wide open.

CHAPTER 7
Abnormal

The following Saturday morning, Billy decided to pay Grandpa Wesley another visit. When he got to the elder's house, the teenager found the usual group of Cherokee people waiting on the porch. Some of them rose from their seats as Billy came near. He greeted them with a polite nod as he moved past them and entered the house. He found Wesley in the kitchen brewing a pot of strong herbal tea.

"What's with the folks on the porch today, Grandpa? They stood up when I arrived."

"They're all waiting for you," Wesley said as he took two coffee cups down from the cupboard. "They all know you're my grandson, and they want to see the boy who saved the children."

"No one was supposed to know about that," Billy said. "The police said they'd keep it quiet."

"The police didn't have anything to do with it," Wesley said as he poured coffee into the two cups. "The bus driver told a couple of his Cherokee friends what happened. And those two Cherokees told ten or so other Cherokees about it. And those ten Cherokees each told another twenty or so Cherokees. You get the picture."

"What do they want from me?"

Wesley put a cup of coffee down on the kitchen table and motioned for Billy to take a seat. Billy sat down.

"There's no question in my mind," Wesley said, taking a sip of the hot liquid. "The Thunders have given you the gift of 'seeing.' Important duties go along with a gift like that."

"But I didn't ask for it," Billy protested, pushing away from the table. "I didn't ask for any of it." A mix of strong feelings rose up inside of him.

"I don't want those kinds of duties." He ran out the back door and into Wesley's garden. He needed to be alone so he could think.

"Is it anger or fear you're feeling?" a familiar voice asked.

"Little Wolf, are you out here somewhere?"

"At your service," the little Indian said, stepping from behind a tall sunflower. "Which is it, anger or fear?"

"I don't know," the boy answered. He calmed down some. "Maybe both," he said.

"That's a good, honest answer," Little Wolf replied with a smile. "There's hope for you yet."

"I'm not so sure." Billy began pacing up and down the path in Wesley's garden. "I see things that normal people don't see. Including short Indians who live in the woods. Some people say I'm gifted. Others say I'm possessed by something evil. My mother thinks I merely suffer from a medical condition."

"You need time to process it all," Little Wolf advised. "You should get back to the morning ritual your grandfather taught you. Quiet your mind and pray to the seven directions. Do you remember what they are?"

Billy stopped pacing to remember.

"Yeah, sure, I remember them."

He pointed to the directions as he described them.

"First there are the four directions—north, south, east, and west. Then there's upward toward Father Sky. That's number five. Then downward to Mother Earth. That's six. Finally, there's inward, into your own heart. That's the seventh direction."

"Good," the little man said. "Placing yourself in the center and praying will help you know what to do. Help you decide which way to go."

This calmed Billy greatly. "Thanks," he said, and he went back inside.

"Grandpa, I'm sorry, but I can't stay to help you today," he said. "Little Wolf said I need time to process everything that's been happening."

"I'm sure he's right," Wesley said. "Why don't you go on home. I'll tell people that you're not up to seeing anyone now. You can leave by the back door."

"Thanks, Grandpa. I knew you'd understand."

Billy spent the rest of the day by himself in the woods. The whispering wind in the nearby trees soothed his mixed-up thoughts. The chirping birds and chattering squirrels blotted out the babble in his brain. And the lone call of a snowy crane calmed his worried mind.

They reminded him that he was related to all things. And all things were related to him.

When he woke up the next morning, his mind was clearer. He went to the backyard and performed the seven-directions ceremony Little Wolf had reminded him about. When he'd finished, he listened quietly to see if any message or sense of direction came. When nothing did, he remembered something else his grandpa had told him.

"This isn't a one-time action you perform and then—boom—you get an answer," Wesley had said. "It's something you do every day to center yourself. It prepares you to be guided. But it takes time."

Feeling calmer and less panicky, Billy decided he would give it time.

He continued seeing the mini-movies and flashes of pictures in his head. But not always. He realized he was only seeing the conflicts or dangers in other people's lives. He wasn't seeing visions of them having quiet family gatherings or happy times with others. He only saw the bad times—the bad times they were causing someone else. The bad times they were getting from someone else.

And he was getting more and more used to it.

But there was one alarming thing he noticed as the week wore on. Oddly, his gym teacher seemed to be growing younger and healthier. Day by day he looked as if he'd been taking some miracle drug. Or drinking some magic energy drink.

Billy knew he wasn't imagining this because Chigger noticed it too.

"I've never seen anyone change like that," Chigger said. "It's like he found the famous fountain of youth or something."

"Now I have even worse feelings about the guy than when I first met him," Billy said. "Something tells me that someone is suffering just so he can look better. Does that make sense?"

"Remember what your grandpa said about your inner voice," Chigger advised. "If you feel that strongly about it, we need to check it out. And by *we,* I mean *you* need to check it out."

"What do you suggest I do?"

"Go up to the man and create an excuse to touch him or hand him something," Chigger said. "There's no other way."

"That's creepy," Billy said with a shiver. "The thought of touching the Birdman creeps me out."

"You got a better idea?"

Billy knew Chigger was right. He'd have to brush up against the guy. Or hand him something so they'd touch it at the same time. He thought hard about it until he came up with a plan.

The next morning before school, Billy ripped his basketball jersey up one side. He showed the tear to Chigger just before gym class.

"At the beginning of class, I'll show Birdman the rip and hand him the jersey," Billy explained. "Hopefully, there'll be a moment when we both touch the cloth."

"That should work," Chigger said. "Good luck."

As they entered the gym, the boys saw Mr. Ravenwood standing near the door to the boys' locker room. Most of the kids in class were headed toward their lockers to put on their basketball outfits. Billy stopped at the doorway. Chigger stayed just behind him to see what would happen.

"Mr. Ravenwood, I've ripped my jersey," Billy said. "Can you get it fixed or give me a new one?" He held the jersey out toward the teacher.

"How in the world did you do that?" the teacher asked sharply. "The now-famous Lightning Boy must really be clumsy." He sighed a big sigh, as if this was such a big deal. "Hand it over so I can take a look."

Birdman reached out for the jersey. Billy put it in the man's hand but didn't let go of it. Both of them had their hands on it for a brief moment. That's when Billy got the familiar mini-jolt that started the movie in his head.

In black and white, he saw a teenage girl tied to a hospital gurney like the one he'd been on in the ambulance. Her mouth was gagged, and she was in a state of panic. The shadowy figure of a man entered the scene. His dark, blurred outline wouldn't come into focus, and he seemed to have bird claws for hands. He drew near the girl with a single claw outstretched toward her. With wide, frightened eyes, the girl squirmed and tried to scream from behind the gag.

The movie ended, and Billy's sight returned to the gym. Mr. Ravenwood was pretending to examine the tear in the jersey, but he was really studying Billy.

"What is it, boy?" the man asked. "You look like you ate something that didn't agree with you."

"No, I *saw* something that didn't agree with me," Billy replied, taking a step away from the teacher. "I saw you threatening a girl who was tied up. You were about to do something bad to her."

A look of shock spread over the Birdman's face. He threw Billy's jersey on the floor and took a quick step toward him.

"I knew there was something wrong with you the minute I laid eyes on you," the angry man barked. "You're not normal. In fact, you're *abnormal*. Something should be done to keep you away from other people."

The teacher quickly stepped into his office and picked up the phone.

"Mr. Sixkiller, this is Ravenwood in the gym," he said into the phone. "The Buckhorn boy is acting strange and needs to be severely disciplined immediately. Probably expelled from school!"

The Birdman listened through the receiver for a moment.

"I'll bring him directly to the office so you can hear the full story." He slammed down the phone and yelled at Billy. "Come with me, weirdo. You're about to find out what the wrath of Ravenwood can do."

Grabbing Billy's shoulder, the teacher pushed the boy toward the principal's office. Again, a movie started running in Billy's head. This time it was in color. He saw Ravenwood opening the trunk of a car. Inside was a dark-skinned teenage Native girl who had been tied up. She was gagged and blindfolded.

Ravenwood picked her up in both arms and carried her toward an abandoned building that seemed familiar to Billy. The girl kicked and struggled and managed to get free of her captor. She fell to the ground but couldn't get up because her feet were tied. The gym teacher reached in his back pocket, pulled out a handgun, and hit the girl in the head with it. She passed out from the blow.

Then the movie stopped. Billy saw that he was now inside the principal's office. The movie had played in his head while they were walking to Mr. Sixkiller's office. The principal rose from his desk.

"I overhead this boy talking to his buddy," Ravenwood said. "He confessed to cutting the brake line on the school bus. It was part of a bigger plan."

"What? That's impossible!" the principal said.

"That's a lie!" Billy responded. "Mr. Ravenwood is a bad man. He's done bad things to kids."

"Whoa, wait a minute," Mr. Sixkiller protested. "This man came highly recommended. He's got a flawless record."

"I think the lightning scrambled his brain," the gym teacher said. "Billy said he made a small cut in the line so the fluid would drain out slowly and not be noticed right away.

Then he jumped on the bus and pretended to save them so he could be called a hero."

"Is this true, Billy?" the principal asked. "I remember that Lieutenant Swimmer said some people in the police force thought you'd cut the line to become more famous."

"No, I didn't mess with the bus," Billy reaffirmed. "I told you how I found out about the brakes. The same way I just found out what this man has been doing. You have to believe me."

"That's just too far-fetched for me," Mr. Sixkiller replied as he reached for his phone. "And this is too difficult for me to figure out. I'm going to let the police sort it out."

Mr. Sixkiller called Lieutenant Swimmer and explained the situation. Then he dismissed the teacher from his office, telling him to make himself available to the police if needed. He told Billy to sit down and wait for the lieutenant to arrive. In the meantime, the principal also called Billy's father to tell him of the latest incident.

Billy was very worried that if no one believed him he'd be spending the night in jail and the Birdman would harm another child.

CHAPTER 8
Proof

"I really want to believe you," Lieutenant Swimmer said as he put Billy in the back seat of his police car. "But your story is pretty wild. You can't go around slandering an upright member of the community that way."

"There has to be some way I can prove it to you," Billy said from the back seat as they headed for the police station. "I am completely innocent, and I believe Mr. Ravenwood is completely guilty. He's probably going to hurt another girl in the very near future."

"And you say you saw this when he touched you?" the lieutenant asked. "Does this supposedly happen whenever you touch someone?"

"Only if that person has been involved in a situation where someone is hurt or in danger," Billy answered. "Or if they're about to be involved in a negative event. At least that seems to be the way it works. I'm still trying to figure it out."

They arrived at the police station and the lieutenant escorted Billy inside. Surprisingly, Little Wolf was lurking in a corner of the waiting room. One of the other officers there, Sergeant Bowers, showed Billy to the conference room.

"Your father is on his way," Sergeant Bowers told Billy. "He'll be present when we talk to you."

As the officer left to get Billy a soda, the little Indian managed to scurry into the room before the door closed.

"What are you doing here?" Billy asked in a whisper.

"Wesley sent me to find you to see if you were all right," Little Wolf said. "He had a vibe that there might be something wrong."

Little Wolf quickly put a finger to his lips to signal Billy to keep quiet. In a few minutes Sergeant Bowers returned with a canned soda and Billy's father.

"Is Billy under arrest?" Mr. Buckhorn asked the officer.

"No," Bowers replied. "We're just trying get a handle on what's really going on. Can I get you anything, Mr. Buckhorn?"

"No, just please move this along as quickly as possible," he replied.

Bowers handed Billy the soda, and both of their hands touched the can briefly. A black-and-white movie began to run in Billy's head. In it the officer was squatted down beside his police car. Someone from inside a nearby old house was shooting at him. When the firing paused, Bowers stood and fired off three quick shots. A scream of pain came from inside the house and the shooting stopped. The movie ended.

"Were you just involved in a shootout?" Billy asked the officer. "With someone inside an old house?"

"Yes, I was," the policeman said. "How did you know that?"

"Yeah, how did you know that?" Billy's dad echoed the question.

"I tried telling you the other day, Dad," Billy answered with frustration. "But you were too fixated on some guy in some historical archive."

Billy turned to Bowers and said, "I just saw an image of it when you handed me the soda can."

"Hold on," Bowers said. "Let me call the lieutenant. He'll want to hear this straight from you."

"I'm sorry I didn't pay more attention," Billy's father said when they were alone. "I didn't think you were serious."

Just then the sergeant returned with Lieutenant Swimmer. Billy described the movie he'd just seen in his head.

"Wait here," the lieutenant said.

The two policemen left the father and son again. What the Buckhorns didn't know was that Swimmer was checking with the others in the station to see if anyone had spoken to the newspaper or radio station about the shootout. No one had. That meant that Billy couldn't have read or heard the story in the news media.

Swimmer and Bowers stepped back into the conference room. Two other uniformed officers came in with them. One was a woman.

"I'd like to introduce officer Frank Barnes and officer Laney Williams," Swimmer said. "Billy, I want you to shake hands with both of them and tell me if you see anything."

Officer Barnes, a white man in his forties, stepped closer to Billy. They shook hands.

Right away a black-and-white mental movie began. Barnes was up in a tree hanging on to a branch. Further out on the branch was a meowing cat. Barnes looked down at an elderly woman on the ground below him. The cat belonged to her.

Then Barnes reached for the cat and lost his balance. Losing his grip, he fell off the branch. In a panic, the officer grabbed for a lower branch and held on. The movie ended.

"It was kind of funny," Billy said with a confident smile. "This man almost fell out of a tree trying to save an elderly woman's cat."

Officer Barnes's jaw dropped. He was greatly surprised.

"That's exactly right," he said. "I nearly broke my leg because of that cat."

Officer Williams, a Native American woman in her thirties, then extended her hand. Billy shook it. This time a color movie played. Williams was leaving a bar at the edge of town called Shooter's Music Tavern. She wasn't in uniform but wore jeans and a Western-style shirt.

Coming from behind a parked car, a very drunk man grabbed Williams. He turned her around and tried to kiss her but missed. In a rapid series of moves, the officer twisted the man's arm and threw him to the ground. Seeing that he was knocked out cold, the woman continued on. The movie stopped.

Billy described the scene and said this event would probably take place sometime in the next few days.

"I was planning on visiting Shooter's tomorrow night," Williams said. "I go a couple of times a month to unwind. I think I'll skip it this time."

"Okay, I've seen enough," Lieutenant Swimmer said. "I don't usually go in for psychics or omens and such, but I believe you're the real thing."

"Boy, am I glad to hear that," Billy said with a sigh.

"I'm speechless," Billy's father admitted. "I didn't believe such things were real."

Little Wolf stepped out from under the conference table and gave Billy a thumbs-up signal. Of course, no one but Billy could see him. The little man left the room to go report Billy's progress to Wesley.

"I think this means your vision of Ravenwood is correct too," Swimmer continued. "It sounds like he's up to no good. But we don't have any real proof to go on."

He paused to think for a moment.

"We'll start doing a background check on Ravenwood and begin an investigation,"

Swimmer said. "I can't go around arresting people based on visions. I have to have solid evidence. Do you understand?"

"Yeah, I get it," Billy replied.

"Of course," Mr. Buckhorn said.

"Billy, you're free to go," Swimmer said. "But don't be surprised if we contact you very soon."

"Sure thing."

"In the meantime, we don't want to tip off Ravenwood that he's being investigated. I'll tell the principal that Billy is in the clear but ask him not to say anything to the gym teacher."

Billy and his dad agreed with the plan.

"I'm late for a meeting I'm in charge of at the college," Mr. Buckhorn said. "Can one of the officers take you back to school to get your truck?"

"I can run him back," Officer Williams said.

"Thanks," Mr. Buckhorn replied. "Billy, I'm sorry for not paying more attention to what you're going through. We can talk some more about it later. Okay?"

"Sure thing, Dad."

Mr. Buckhorn patted his son on the back and left the station.

After Williams dropped off Billy at the high school, the boy drove out to Grandpa's house. As he moved through the countryside, he thought about what had been going on. It all seemed too strange to be true. How could such things happen to a backwoods Cherokee teenager? He really wanted no part of it. But he also wanted to talk to somebody about it.

At his grandpa's, Billy found a note stuck to the front door. "Gone to the woods to gather medicine," the note read. "Won't be back for a few hours."

Then Billy drove home to see if his mother had gotten back from work. He found a note from her stuck on the refrigerator door that read, "Running errands—fix yourself a snack. Be back in time for dinner."

He decided to call his dad to find out when he'd be home. "I'm in meetings until at least eight o'clock tonight," his voice-mail message said. "Leave a message." Billy hung up without saying anything.

Why couldn't he find someone when he needed to talk? When he needed to vent? Billy even looked around to see if Little Wolf was lurking anywhere, but there was no sign of the little man. He had probably joined Wesley in the woods after leaving the police station.

Billy realized that the mini-jolts and the movies in his head had drained him of energy. So he decided to take a nap. Flopping down on his bed, he soon fell asleep.

But it was not a peaceful sleep. In a vivid dream, he saw a girl being tied up by a man inside a darkened cabin. In the background, he saw two other girls. They had already been tied and gagged. They looked drugged or dazed.

At first he couldn't see who the man was. Within the dream, he forced himself to look up to see the man's face. He began getting a headache and the images started to fade. But somehow Billy willed the dream to continue. He willed it to show him what he needed to see.

With great effort he was able to tilt his view far enough upward to see the back of the man's head. At that moment, the man became aware that Billy was looking at him. The man turned his face away from the girl, and his angry eyes met Billy's. It was Ravenwood! Rage filled the man's face, and his human face changed into the face of a black-feathered raven with dark, piercing eyes!

Then the gym teacher's whole body changed into a large raven. He became an enraged bird that flew toward Billy, squawking and flapping and clawing at him. The shock of the image jolted Billy out of the dream and back into his room. He sat upright in bed, feeling hot and sweaty but at the same time cold and clammy.

This seemed like more than a dream. More than a nightmare. It felt like his very soul had crossed over into another place. Somewhere between the land of the living and the land of the dead. Was this a real event happening now or was it something that might happen in the future? Did Ravenwood actually see Billy during the dream? These were questions with no answers.

And this wasn't something he could tell anyone except maybe Grandpa. No one would believe it. He wasn't sure he believed it himself. He had learned from Grandpa that some powerful medicine men, both good and evil, could transform themselves into animals. Birds or dogs usually. They did this so they could travel without being recognized. The good ones did it to check up on their own patients. And the bad ones did it to spy on people they wanted to harm.

But Ravenwood was a white man, Billy remembered. *Where did he learn these secret Cherokee medicine skills?*

Billy checked his pocket watch and saw that it was time for school to let out. He decided to go visit Chigger to see what, if anything, had happened there the rest of the day. Chigger and his family lived in a trailer home parked at the end of a long gravel driveway east of town.

"My parents told me I can't hang out with you anymore," Chigger said when he answered his front door. "The gossip around town has gone viral. People are making all kinds of strange claims against you."

Chigger stepped out on the porch so his mother wouldn't see that it was Billy he was talking to. He closed the door behind him quietly.

"It's like Bigfoot sightings," the boy continued. "People are saying they've seen you doing all kinds of shady things all over the place. It's not even possible for one person to be in all those places at the same time." That statement caused Chigger to begin wondering. "Is it?" he added.

"How long have we been friends?" Billy asked, disturbed that his own friend was doubting him. "How long have your parents known me?" He pulled at the ends of his hair, something he did when he was stressed.

"I know, I know," Chigger replied. "It's totally bogus. But what can I do? My father rules the family with an iron hand. And Mom's too scared of him to argue or disagree. So here I sit like a rabbit in a trap."

Feelings of hurt, betrayal, and anger grew inside Billy. He paced back and forth on Chigger's porch. He spoke more to himself than to Chigger.

"A few days ago everyone wanted to meet the boy who saved the kids on the bus. Now people think I'm some kind of dangerous freak. What's going on?"

"Keep your voice down or my parents will hear you," Chigger said.

Billy stopped pacing and faced Chigger with hurt, angry eyes.

"Of all people, I thought I could at least count on you, Chigger!" he yelled and turned away.

Storming off the porch, Billy ran back to his truck. He put the gear in reverse and sped backward out of the gravel driveway. Bits of gravel flew up from the spinning tires and pelted Chigger in the face and arms. Knowing that he'd let down his best friend, Chigger watched as Billy disappeared down the road.

How would he ever fix this? Chigger wondered.

CHAPTER 9
Turning Point

When he got home, Billy started pulling out his camping gear from his closet. *It is time to head for the woods,* he thought. *Time to surround myself with earth and sky and trees and nature. Maybe they could help now.*

It was his turn to leave behind notes and messages for others to find. He left one note on the refrigerator to his mother. "Gone to the woods to be alone," it read. "I won't be back in time for dinner." He left another note on his dad's desk upstairs. "Gone to connect with the real me," this one read. "I can't be the person others want me to be."

With gear and food in the truck, he hitched up his boat trailer and headed south. Down State Highway 82 he went, toward one of his favorite places on earth, Lake Tenkiller.

The huge body of water had more than one hundred miles of shoreline. Plenty of room to get away.

He threw his camping equipment and some food into the skiff and backed it into the water at a public boat area he'd used many times before. After parking his truck in the nearby lot, he pointed the boat toward an island that he and Chigger had discovered awhile back. At the time, they thought it might even be the island where the Thunders had sent Fire down to earth.

Shaped like an arrowhead, the tree-covered chunk of land was not much bigger than a football field. But it was surrounded by acres and acres of lake. It was isolated from the camping and fishing sites used by normal people.

But he wasn't normal, was he? He had been declared abnormal. And for some reason, that was how people had come to think of him. *So be it,* he thought. *I'll just see what being abnormal is all about.*

The flat-bottom boat touched the island's rocky shore. Grabbing his gear, he stepped out and into the shallow water. A few tugs had the boat up on dry land. He tied the bow rope to a tree stump and hiked inland.

Locating a small hill near the middle of the island, he dropped his gear on the ground. He decided he'd tour his temporary home to make sure it didn't hold any surprises. He didn't want to be visited by a wildcat or black bear that might be living there.

Once that had been done, he set up camp and built a fire. And as darkness settled in, he was feeling right at home. He cooked the ideal outdoor dinner for himself over the fire. It was a campfire creation his grandpa called "cowboy stew." All that was required was a can of beef stew and a can of ranch beans. Pour them both into a cast iron kettle and set it into the coals. A few minutes later you had the heartiest meal west of the Mississippi. And a few minutes after that, you only had one pot and one spoon to clean. Billy used water from the five-gallon jug he'd brought to do that job.

Once again a star-filled sky floated overhead. Billy rolled out his sleeping bag next to the fire and slipped into it. Above him were spread out the animal star groups known to the Cherokee. The stars were the spirit campfires of the Star People, according to Grandpa. They would keep him company this night.

A shooting star raced across the sky above him. It was a sign of a coming change. At least that's what Grandpa said it meant. But Billy was beginning to question his grandfather's teachings. Those quaint old ideas about how things worked in the world. Maybe those were just the fantasies of old men and little boys. That's what floated through Billy's mind as he drifted off to sleep.

Billy slipped into a deep, peaceful slumber. It was like his coma in the hospital after the lightning strike. Blurry stories swirled around him in the night. At one point Billy seemed to be flying over the land looking down. He passed over the nearby plant nursery, with its greenhouses and rows of dead plants. It has been closed down for years. And later he saw a whole group of Little People dancing around a fire.

When he awoke the following morning, he took a moment to remember the dream images from the night before. As he got up, he somehow felt lighter and his head felt clearer than when he'd gone to bed. The feelings of betrayal and anger were gone. A new sense of comfort had settled over him in his sleep. But he didn't know where it came from.

That's because he didn't know that Wesley had spent the entire night doctoring him from afar with Cherokee songs and prayers. When Billy's mom and dad discovered the notes he had left for them, they called Wesley and asked for his help. And for the first time in a long time, Wesley turned to Little Wolf and the other Little People for their very special help.

Together they held an all-night stomp dance in the field behind Wesley's house to conjure the power and vision that Billy would need in the days ahead. For they knew a battle between the Dark and the Light was brewing in the Cherokee Nation.

Back on the island, just after sunrise, Billy prayed to the seven directions. He was truly grateful that the bad feelings he had felt the day before had left him. His thankfulness was part of this morning's message to the rising sun.

Afterward, he packed up his gear and cleaned up his campsite. Carrying his trash with him, he shoved his skiff from the shore and cranked up the engine. He'd decided it was time for him to firmly take the next step on that ladder. The ladder he'd seen in his vision at the stomp dance made more sense to him now.

He drove back home as quickly as he could and unhitched the boat. Walking toward his house, he was surprised to find his father sitting on the front porch with Lieutenant Swimmer. His father was usually headed for his teaching job at the college by this time of morning. He and the lieutenant were talking quietly and seriously while looking at an open file folder.

"Are you all right?" Billy's father asked, rising from his chair. "You had us worried sick."

"I'm just fine," Billy replied, hugging his dad. "More than fine. And I'm sorry I worried you. I just needed some time to sort a few things out."

Looking at Lieutenant Swimmer, he asked, "What's going on?"

"Yesterday, after you left our office, we began trying to gather information on Ravenwood," Swimmer said. "We went back to the high school to interview him, but he'd left. We looked for him at the address the school had for him, but he wasn't there either."

"Maybe he was just out running errands or something," Billy's dad offered.

"The odd thing is that there was just a boarded up old house at that address," the lieutenant replied. "It looked like it hadn't been lived in for years. Ravenwood seems to have disappeared."

He handed the open file folder to Billy.

"And so has this girl," Swimmer said.

He pointed to the photo of a teenage girl clipped to the inside of the folder. "Her mother called us and said she didn't come home after school yesterday."

Billy looked at the photo and realized that the girl looked familiar. She was a dark-skinned Native girl with striking green eyes. Did he know her from one of his classes?

"Her name is Sara Cornsilk," Swimmer continued. "She's a student at your school."

"I guess I've seen her around," Billy said. Then he remembered where he'd seen her.

"Wait. I saw her yesterday afternoon in a weird, scary dream I had," Billy said with excitement as he recalled the images. "The gym teacher was taking her out of the trunk of a car and carrying her into an old empty building."

"You saw this yesterday?" Swimmer asked.

"Yes, and it was in color," Billy confirmed. "That means it hadn't happened yet." He thought about it for another moment, and then added, "But it could have happened later in the day."

"Can you tell me more about the building you saw in your vision?" the lieutenant inquired.

Billy searched his memory.

"Not really," Billy said. "That wasn't clear in my dream. But it did seem like it was an old warehouse or office building. It seemed familiar, but I'm not sure."

"So we've got two people we need to find and fast," Swimmer said. "I hope you're wrong about this, Billy. But I'm afraid you might be right."

With that the officer hurried back to his police car and sped away.

"I'll call your mother and let her know you're back," Mr. Buckhorn said. "Are you going to school today?"

"I don't think so," Billy replied. "I need to do something to help find Ravenwood before he does anything to that girl."

"It sounds too dangerous," his father said. "Why don't you let the police handle it?"

"Because I feel like it's my duty somehow," Billy answered. "It seems like it's time for me to step up and begin to follow in Grandpa's footsteps."

With those words, Mr. Buckhorn fell silent. He knew that someday his son would say those words. He knew that someday the seeds of ancient stories, beliefs, and practices would sprout in the fertile soil of his soul. These seeds had been planted by Billy's grandmother and grandfather. But Billy's father just didn't think this day would arrive so soon.

"It's not an easy path, you know," Mr. Buckhorn said.

"I know."

"But if you feel the calling, I won't prevent you from following that path," Billy's father said. He paused and looked into his son's eyes. They seemed deep and mature for a sixteen-year-old. "What's next then?"

"What else?" Billy said. "Go see Grandpa. You know he's the best in three counties at finding lost people and things."

"What about school?" his father asked.

"I've got more important things to tend to right now," Billy said.

"Good luck—and stay safe," his father said, kissing his son on the top of his head. "As always, I've got to get back to the college."

As he walked to his car, Billy's dad was worried. Was his son destined to get caught up in the strange world of Cherokee medicine? It was a world filled with mysterious events and happenings. For the first time, he realized that it could also be dangerous.

As Billy walked to his truck, he wished Chigger was with him. Billy had always been a bit more adventurous than his friend. But it was really part of an act. Pretending to be braver than Chigger is what had often given Billy the courage to embark on an adventure in the first place.

CHAPTER 10
The Raven Stalker

Billy drove to Wesley's house as fast as he could. He had a lot to tell the old man and a lot to ask of him. When he arrived, he found his grandfather's truck parked in the front yard. The front door to the house was open and Billy stepped inside.

"Grandpa," he called several times as he searched inside the house. No reply came. He stepped into the backyard and called again. Still no reply. And a quick search didn't locate Little Wolf either.

What's going on, Billy thought. *Why are people disappearing?*

Then he heard a moan coming from a row of sunflowers growing in the back of Wesley's garden. Billy ran toward the sound. There he found his grandfather sprawled on the ground. His head was bloody and seemed to be covered with stab wounds.

"Grandpa, what happened?" the panicked boy cried. "Are you all right?"

Wesley struggled to speak. His words were weak.

"I was attacked by a raven, a large one," the wounded elder said between breaths.

"Don't try to talk," Billy cautioned. "Save your strength."

"No, this is important!" Wesley said, gathering all his energy. "It's a Shape-Changer, Billy, a Raven Stalker. He must be stopped, no matter what."

He then passed out. Billy ran inside to call his mother at the hospital.

"We'll send out an ambulance," she said. "Wait right there."

"No, I'm bringing him in myself," Billy protested. "It'll take too long for an ambulance to get here. Just have everything ready when I get there." He hung up before she could say no.

Billy drove his truck around the side of Wesley's house and into the back. He knocked a hole in the garden fence and backed the pickup close to his grandfather. From inside the house he brought out some blankets and spread them in the bed of the truck. Somehow, with a burst of superhuman strength, he lifted the wounded elder up and into the truck. With the bungee cords he used to tie down cargo, Billy strapped Wesley in so he wouldn't bounce around.

Breaking every speeding law in the Cherokee Nation, he raced to the hospital. Thankfully, his mother had emergency room staff standing by. They wheeled Billy's grandpa into the ER and began working on him. Billy had to stay out in the waiting room.

About a half hour later, Billy's dad joined him. Billy told him how he'd found Wesley in the garden with his head and hands covered in blood and stab wounds.

"That's the strangest thing I've ever heard," Mr. Buckhorn said. "How did something like that even happen?"

"Grandpa said it was a Shape-Changer, a kind of witch known as a Raven Stalker," Billy answered. "I think the bird stabbed Grandpa with his beak over and over again."

Mr. Buckhorn sat speechless. He knew his father was a medicine man, a healer. His mother had been one too. But he'd never believed that anything dangerous would ever come of it. And Billy wanted to follow in his grandparents' footsteps. Maybe that wasn't such a good idea after all.

A doctor who was removing his surgical face mask and gloves came out of the operating room. He walked toward Billy and his father.

"It's not as bad as it looks," the man reported. "Head wounds sometimes bleed more heavily than similar wounds in other parts of the body."

"Can we see him?" Mr. Buckhorn asked.

"Yes, very briefly. But he specially asked to see his grandson first," the doctor said. "He said he needs to talk with him about things that concern a medicine man and his apprentice."

"Sorry, Dad," Billy said, as he followed the doctor down the hall. "I'll try to make it quick."

The doctor led Billy to his grandfather's room and left him to enter alone. The boy opened the door to the room and found his grandfather lying in bed. Tubes were attached to him. Wesley's head was wrapped in gauze bandages and so were his hands.

"Grandpa, what's going on? You told me Raven Stalkers were a thing of the past. Now you say one just attacked you."

"It was the dark, shriveled soul of Benjamin Blacksnake," Wesley said with great weariness. "He lived among the Eastern Cherokees in North Carolina. He died in 1964."

Billy blinked a few times. He didn't understand.

"He was a well-known Raven Stalker in his day," Grandpa continued. "Bad medicine through and through. Raven Stalkers visit sick people who are near death and drain them of their last bit of life. The person would die, but the Raven Stalker would be strengthened and able to add years to his own life."

"Why is he here now?"

"Blacksnake's evil spirit took possession of your Mr. Ravenwood," Wesley answered. "He's living here in our world through your gym teacher's body. He probably took over the teacher's life back in North Carolina before coming here."

"How do you know all this?"

"He identified himself to me just before he attacked," Grandpa replied. "He'd become aware that I was getting close to discovering the source of the evil your grandma warned us about. Using his remote viewing powers, he found me and made his move."

The doctor stepped back into the room and said, "That's enough for now. He needs to rest."

Reluctantly, Billy stood to leave. "One more thing," he said loud enough for the doctor to hear. Then he leaned in close to his grandfather and whispered, "If an evil dead medicine man is controlling Ravenwood and using him to kidnap kids . . . how do we stop him?"

Grandpa let out a big, mournful sigh and looked up at Billy.

"That's beyond my skills, I'm sorry to say," he said.

Billy gently touched his grandfather's arm.

"Then I'll take it from here," he told Wesley. "You get well." He turned and left the room before his grandfather could say anything else.

Of course, Billy couldn't tell anybody what Wesley had told him. It sounded like the delusions of a crazy old man, not to be taken seriously. Billy drove directly to the police station to talk to Lieutenant Swimmer. He had to convince the man that Ravenwood was definitely dangerous and able to hurt anyone who got in his way. And he had to do it without saying anything about Raven Stalkers or dead medicine men.

The receptionist at the police station, Mrs. Atwood, said that the lieutenant and most of the officers were in the field searching for the missing girl.

"You have to tell Lieutenant Swimmer that he needs to focus on finding Ravenwood," Billy said. "He's got the girl somewhere, and he's more dangerous than anyone realizes."

Mrs. Atwood assured him that she would give Swimmer that message, but Billy wasn't sure she would follow through.

Then he drove to the high school to find the principal, Mr. Sixkiller.

"Mr. Ravenwood is *not* the upstanding member of the community you think he is," Billy told him. "Someone from his last job must have lied when they endorsed him for the gym teacher job."

"Why aren't you in class, young man?" the principal said, ignoring Billy's statement. "You were reported absent from school this morning."

"Didn't Lieutenant Swimmer call you yesterday?" Billy asked impatiently.

"Why, yes, he did, but—"

"And didn't he tell you that Ravenwood is now under investigation?"

"Yes, but I don't see—"

"And didn't he tell you that I'm in the clear?"

"Yes. Yes, he did."

"So I don't have time to play games," Billy said, his impatience growing. "I'm helping the police track down Ravenwood. He's a dangerous man who does bad things to kids."

"Do you have proof?"

"Yes, and you can talk to Lieutenant Swimmer if you don't believe me," Billy replied with authority. "Now, who did Ravenwood's recommendation come from?"

"Well, our own gym teacher, Mr. Wildcat, recommended Ravenwood after he got sick," the principal answered. "I didn't speak to him, but Mr. Wildcat sent me an email just before Labor Day. It said he was very sick and would not be able to teach this semester."

"Please give me Mr. Wildcat's home address and phone number so the police can talk to him," Billy requested. "He may have some clues about who Ravenwood really is."

Sixkiller hesitated for a moment. He was not sure that a sixteen-year-old should be involved in a police matter. Billy could see that the principal had his doubts.

"I'm not comfortable sharing this information with a student," the principal said.

"Look, Mr. Sixkiller, my grandpa is laid up in the hospital with severe stab wounds," the boy said. "He says Ravenwood was his attacker. The police are searching for him and a missing student as we speak. So any delays could mean injury or death for that girl."

This information shook Sixkiller to the bone.

"I hope I don't regret doing this later," the principal said.

He opened a nearby filing cabinet and looked through the folders. He found Mr. Wildcat's file and took it to his desk. Grabbing a piece a paper from a drawer, he quickly scribbled an address and phone number.

"I hope you're wrong about this," Mr. Sixkiller said as he handed the paper to Billy. "But if you're right, I'll be the first to back you up. Go get him, son."

Billy took the paper and left.

CHAPTER 11
Shape-Changer

Billy decided *not* to go to the police station with Mr. Wildcat's address and phone number. He thought it would take too long for the police to check it out. He felt a real sense of urgency about it. So he drove to the address himself. He was following his inner vision.

The house at that address was a two-story log home similar to his own. But Mr. Wildcat's yard had been neglected for a while. The grass was tall. The front flower garden was overgrown with weeds. Mail overflowed from the front porch mailbox, too.

Billy rang the doorbell and waited. No one stirred. He knocked loudly on the door and again waited. Still no response. He peeked into the house through a front window. The house was dark. Nothing moved.

He decided to take a look at the back of the house and called out several times as he walked: "Mr. Wildcat, are you there? Hello. Is anyone home?"

He reached the back door and found it slightly open. He looked around outside to make sure no one was watching. He stepped inside. He found himself in the kitchen, surrounded by the foul odor of stale and rotting food. It was dark, so he flipped on a light switch. No lights came on.

Moving through the room, Billy discovered half-empty containers of take-out food scattered around. On the kitchen table and on the counters sat pizza boxes, burger bags, and sacks from three or four other local restaurants.

"Mr. Wildcat, are you here?" he called out again. Still no answer. Moving out of the kitchen and into the living room, he noticed a partially opened side door. It might take him to a basement, he thought. He flipped on a light switch located on the wall just inside the door. The basement light came on, and right away he heard what sounded like a person moaning loudly.

Cautiously, he made his way down the creaky wooden stairs that led to the basement. He wasn't prepared for the sight that greeted him at the bottom of the stairs. A blindfolded man lay strapped to a hospital gurney. He was trying to scream through the gag that had been tied over his mouth. And he was trying urgently to break free of his restraints.

Billy ran to the man, slipped off the blindfold, and pulled down the gag. It was Mr. Wildcat. He was alive, but his hollow eyes were sunken. His body was nothing but skin and bones. He could barely speak.

"Thank God someone finally came," he said weakly. "I don't think I could've held on much longer."

"Mr. Wildcat, who did this to you?" Billy asked as he removed the straps.

"That whacked-out monster Ravenwood," he replied as he tried to sit up. "He showed up on my doorstep right after school started in August. He tied me up and put me down here. He sent an email to Mr. Sixkiller pretending to be me. It said that I was too sick to teach this semester. He even lied about knowing me and gave himself a reference for the job under my name."

"I wondered how he pulled that off," Billy said. "Let's get you to the hospital right away."

He grabbed the man to help him stand. Before they could take a step together, a black-and-white movie began to run in Billy's head. He saw Mr. Wildcat tied to this gurney here in the basement. Ravenwood entered and began chanting a strange song. It sounded like some sort of ancient form of the Cherokee language. He drank a dark liquid from a glass that sat on a nearby shelf. In a moment, he began to change into a raven—a huge, oversized version of a raven. Then the movie stopped.

"Grandpa was right," Billy said, more to himself than to Mr. Wildcat.

"What?" the gym teacher asked.

"Nothing," Billy replied.

He helped the man get outside and into his truck's extended cab. The teacher lay down in the back seat, using a blanket for a pillow. During the drive to the hospital, Mr. Wildcat revealed more details about his ordeal.

"You'll probably think I'm nuts, but I swear I saw Ravenwood transform into a bird—a big, weird raven," Mr. Wildcat said. He watched Billy and waited for a response.

"You don't have to convince me," Billy replied. "Just now I saw a movie in my head of him in the middle of his shape-change. The man's been possessed by the evil spirit of a dead medicine man."

That response surprised and shocked the teacher, who was used to normal, everyday reality, not the workings of the supernatural.

"What else happened?" Billy asked.

"One day, I was tied down to the gurney and he flew up above me," the teacher said. "He flapped his huge wings and then landed on my chest. I was so scared that he was going to eat me or something."

"He's what my grandfather calls a Raven Stalker," Billy told him. "They feed on your life force, not your flesh."

"That explains it," Mr. Wildcat said, thinking about what had happened to him. "He seemed to be strengthened by my fear. A shiver passed through him as he soaked it up. Then he stuck his beak in my mouth and began sucking. The more he sucked, the weaker I felt. He'd return every few days for another feeding. Then he'd give me just enough food and water to keep me alive."

"Did he say where else he was going besides the high school?"

"Not really," the weakening teacher answered. "He said he came to eastern Oklahoma to be where everything is green. He liked to be away from town at a place where water, earth, plants, and sky all came together." His voice trickled off to a whisper near the end of his sentence. Billy knew he'd better step on it to get the man to a doctor before it was too late.

"Keep this up and we'll have to give you a job as an ambulance driver," the receiving nurse in the emergency room said. "Who have you got this time?"

"This is Mr. Wildcat, the high school gym teacher," Billy said. "And he may need the help of a medicine man in addition to what you can do for him. He's been under the spell of what you'd call a witch. Now I've got to report this to the police and visit my grandpa, who's on another floor."

Using the phone at the nurse's station, Billy called the police station and got Mrs. Atwood again.

"Did you give Lieutenant Swimmer my message?" Billy asked. He could tell she was filing her fingernails.

"Well, he's been kinda busy, and there's other stuff goin' on here, so—"

"Look, lady," Billy interrupted. "You need to quit focusing on your cosmetic concerns and put me through to Swimmer!" Before she could respond, he added, "I found Mr. Wildcat, the gym teacher, and he was nearly dead."

"I thought Ravenwood was the gym teacher," the woman replied, putting down the fingernail file. "And you'd better watch yourself, mister. That's no way to talk to law enforcement personnel."

Billy contained his anger as best he could.

"Please get Lieutenant Swimmer on the radio, ma'am, or patch me through to him. Whatever you have to do. Because he needs to hear what Mr. Wildcat, the original gym teacher, had to say."

Reluctantly, the receptionist called the lieutenant on her police radio. When he came on the line, she connected Billy to his radio. He quickly gave his report about the attack on Wesley and the discovery of Mr. Wildcat in the basement.

"That's good work, young man," the lieutenant said. "Keep this up and we'll have to put you on the police force."

"No thanks. I've already been offered a job driving ambulances today. Have you got any ideas about where this maniac is hiding out?"

"We've begun searching for abandoned properties, since that's the only clue we have so far. We've called in the sheriff's department to help us out. The area we need to cover is huge."

"Please let me know if you come up with anything," Billy said. "I'm going back to visit my grandpa."

They ended the call and Billy took the elevator up to Wesley's room.

"He's not finished with me," Grandpa Wesley said, sitting up in his bed. "I can feel Blacksnake or Ravenwood or whatever you want to call him." He spoke between bites of chocolate pudding that came from a lunch tray beside his bed. "He's out there somewhere. I can't see him, but I feel like he's circling overhead."

Billy looked out the window and scanned the sky, but he didn't see any signs of an oversized raven.

"I'll keep an eye out for him," Billy said. "The police are searching empty buildings outside town, but there are so many. It'll be tough to find the right one."

"You can find him," Wesley said with confidence. "You have the power, but it just hasn't been developed yet. It takes practice and time."

Billy gave his grandpa a gentle hug and said, "I'll do my best."

Then he left. He took the elevator down to the main floor and walked out to his truck, which was parked in the hospital's lot. He thought more about what his grandfather had told him. *You can find him. You have the power.*

Just then a shadow passed over Billy's face. He looked up and spied a rather large black bird flying overhead.

"Ravenwood!" Billy said out loud with excitement.

He continued watching the bird as it headed south. Billy jumped in his truck and sped off in the same direction. He tried to keep sight of the bird as he drove. Sometimes it was through the front windshield. Other times he had to poke his head out the rolled-down driver's-side window. The bird flew straight, but Billy had to zig-zag down the streets to follow it.

Before long, he was out of town and heading south on State Highway 82. *That's the road to Lake Tenkiller,* Billy thought.

He drove down the highway with one eye on the road and the other eye on the raven. After about fifteen minutes, the bird started losing altitude. Billy saw it come in for a landing ahead of him, not too far from the western shore of the lake.

"So he's been hiding out at the old abandoned plant nursery all this time," Billy said out loud. "Why couldn't I see that before?"

He turned his truck off the highway and into the back entrance to the nursery. There was usually a locked chain across that entrance, but it had been cut. Driving slowly through the grounds, Billy scanned the rows of dead plants and shrubs. He looked for any movement. He saw nothing.

The empty buildings, rundown equipment, decaying plants, and dead trees gave the place an eerie feeling. *What a perfect place for the dried-up soul of an evil medicine man to hide out,* he thought.

In a few minutes he came to the nursery's main building, located in the center of the property. A car was parked near the front door of that building. Billy recognized the car. It was the one he'd seen in his nightmare vision when Ravenwood took Sara Cornsilk out of his trunk.

Billy then flashed back to memories of the place when he and Chigger used to play there as young kids. Chigger's dad supervised the workers who took care of the plants. Sometimes on a Saturday, he and Chigger went to work with his dad. They played hide-

and-seek among the greenhouses and rows of plants.

I wish you were with me now, Chigger, Billy thought.

He knew that Sara was in danger, so he needed to take action. Again he decided there wasn't time to call in the police. He'd have to check it out himself.

Moving as quietly as he could, Billy parked his truck and stepped inside the building's main entrance. It was dimly lit inside, and he had to wait for his eyes to adjust. The front area used to be a waiting room, but it was empty now. Behind the waiting room was the first of many warehouse growing rooms.

Billy took two quiet steps into the first warehouse room and suddenly felt a cool spray of mist cover his face. For a moment, he smelled the sweet fragrance of flowers. Then he passed out and fell to the floor.

Billy didn't know how long he'd been out. He was just waking up when he heard a raspy voice say, "You're not as clever as you think you are, Lightning Boy."

Billy opened his eyes to find that he was tied securely to an office chair that had little wheels. He was in a darkened warehouse that smelled of manure and rotting plants. He blinked several times, trying to become used to the dimly lit room.

"I was the one who spread those nasty rumors about you," the raspy voice continued. "Small-town people are so trusting when it comes to gossip."

Ravenwood stepped into Billy's line of sight. Or was it Ravenwood? As Billy watched, the outline of the figure seemed to blur and shift. One moment he looked like Ravenwood. The next moment he looked like someone else, a shriveled old Indian man. Mixed in there was also the fuzzy image of a large bird with beady black eyes.

"And now you've stepped right into my trap," the Birdman said. "You've arrived just in time to witness the entire glorious process. I've been saving the girl until you showed up. And I'm sure you'll enjoy the show."

The constantly changing thing stepped back into the darkness. A moment later there came a loud click from behind Billy. Lights came on in another area of the warehouse. In the middle of the lighted space was a gurney that had Sara strapped to it. Her head was covered with a cloth sack.

Ravenwood wheeled Billy's chair across the floor until he was within a few feet of Sara. Then the Birdman stepped over to the gurney and removed the sack. Sara's mouth was taped shut. She jerked and tried in vain to break free of her bonds.

"The first step is to spark fear into your subject's heart," the Birdman said. "You've heard the saying 'we have nothing to fear but fear itself.' Well, in this case, it's very true. Fear is such a delicious energy. I like to start a soul meal with fear as the appetizer."

The Birdman picked up a large knife from a table close to the gurney. He licked the blade as though it held the juice of a tasty piece of food. He turned the blade back and forth to catch the light and reflect it onto Sara's face.

Billy saw Sara's eyes fly wide open in fear. That was the reaction Ravenwood was after. He bent his face down near hers and took in a deep breath.

Billy's vision had somehow been enhanced. Maybe the mist sprayed into his face had done this. He could actually see the fear energy glowing out from Sara. Then, when the Birdman breathed in, he could see that cloud of fear get sucked into his nostrils.

It was easy to see that Ravenwood gained strength from Sara's fear. He stood tall and erect. Then he turned an angry gaze toward Billy. This time when he spoke, there was no sign of the raspy voice.

"When you meddled in my affairs and warned that bus driver about the dangerous bus, you robbed me of a glorious feast!" The Birdman closed his eyes and thought about what he'd missed out on that day. "The fear I would have tasted that day could have fed me for weeks."

He opened his angry eyes and vented his fury at Billy.

"But you had to go and spoil everything! You've interfered with my plans once too often!"

As the anger bubbled up from inside Ravenwood, he began changing. His shifting outline took the form of the old Indian. Billy guessed that this was the true form of Benjamin Blacksnake, the entity guilty for all of this.

"Your grandpa got what was coming to him," Blacksnake barked. The raspy voice had returned. "And after I'm finished with the girl here, you'll get what's coming to you."

Blacksnake began chanting the summons he'd used on Mr. Wildcat. Another change began as the old man turned into an oversized raven. When the change was complete, he spread his wings and rose up into the overhead space near the warehouse rafters.

He then swooped down, landing on Sara's chest. Sticking his beak into her mouth, the bird began sucking the life force from her.

Billy struggled to free himself of the rope that kept him tied to his chair. When that didn't work, he realized he could scoot the chair across the floor on its wheels. While the Raven Stalker was focused on Sara, Billy pushed himself off a support post and hurled himself backward toward the gurney.

He slammed into the gurney with the back of the chair and succeeded in knocking the bird off Sara and onto the floor. This enraged the Shape-Changer, and he directed his wrath toward Billy.

Having seen what the Raven Stalker could do with a person's fear, Billy controlled himself enough to keep fear from rising up in him. Instead, he channeled that energy into anger. He needed to fight the Birdman's anger with his own.

"Come and get me, Birdman," Billy screamed. "I'm not afraid of you."

CHAPTER 12
The Hideout

Chigger really missed hanging out with his best friend. They'd known each other since first grade. And now he was forbidden to see Billy because of some silly rumors. That's all they were. Rumors that said Billy cut the school bus brake lines. Rumors that said Billy was just trying to get publicity and become famous. Rumors that said Billy was having delusions. That he imagined he could see people's past or future.

Chigger felt he needed to get away and clear his head. He decided to borrow his dad's car to take a drive. He wanted to go visit one of the places where he and Billy played as kids. The Greenhouse Plant and Tree Nursery had been a very active business once upon a time. His father supervised the workers then. He remembered that the nursery went out of business years ago when the economy was bad.

Driving south through the wooded hills on State Highway 82, Chigger arrived at the back gate to the nursery in a short twenty minutes. He and Billy had sometimes come in through this gate after the place had been shut down. No one really watched this entrance.

Chigger turned his dad's car off the main road near the gate. He expected the entrance to have a chain across it to keep people out. But the chain had been cut and was lying in the dirt.

He drove down the narrow back road that led to the middle of the property. As he looked at the rows of dead plants and empty greenhouses, he thought of the days when he and Billy had free run through the place. Catching bugs, running foot races, and playing hide-and-seek were the games of those days. They even played cowboys and Indians, but Billy always got to be the Indian.

As he reached the center of the property, he saw Billy's pickup truck parked in front of the main building. Another car was parked beside it. *Why is Billy's truck way out here?* he wondered.

Chigger thought hard for a minute. He knew the police were on a manhunt for Mr. Ravenwood. He'd heard that Billy's grandpa had been hurt in some weird attack. He knew that Wesley was teaching Billy the medicine ways of the Cherokee, things that were over Chigger's head. Then a thought struck him. *Could this be where Ravenwood is hiding out? And could Billy have discovered that?*

He looked more closely at the car parked beside Billy's truck. It had a sticker on the back windshield that read "High School Faculty." That meant it was definitely a teacher's car. He peered into the back seat through a side window. The inside of the car was littered with food wrappers, gym clothes, and file boxes.

Chigger tried the back-door handle and found it unlocked. Opening the door, he reached into the nearest file box and pulled out what looked like a very old book. It had a worn leather cover and was bound with leather strips. He opened it and flipped through it.

Page after page and line after line was handwritten in the Cherokee language. Chigger knew from his class in tribal history that this language had been invented by Sequoyah in the 1800s. Along with the words were crude drawings that showed plants and healing methods. With the little knowledge he had of the subject, Chigger realized that this was one of the ancient books of Cherokee medicine. It was something a medicine man like Wesley might use. And he also realized that what he had stumbled into was probably dangerous and beyond his understanding. It was time to call the police or the sheriff or *somebody.*

He closed the car door, jumped in his dad's car, and sped away. He knew that just up the road was a gas station that had a phone.

Chigger didn't have a cell phone. Neither did Billy. A few years back, Billy's teenage cousin on his dad's side, Jason, was in a serious car wreck. The accident left him paralyzed from the waist down. He had been using his cell phone while driving. Ever since then, Mr. Buckhorn forbid Billy to have a cell phone until he turned eighteen. Chigger's parents liked the idea and did the same with him. The boys regularly used public phones.

In a matter of minutes he was on the phone and dialing the police station, a phone number his father made him memorize in case of emergencies.

As usual, Mrs. Atwood answered the phone. But she had been scolded by her boss. She now understood that anything having to do with Billy Buckhorn had top priority. When Chigger mentioned where he'd found Billy's truck, the woman shifted into high gear and alerted Lieutenant Swimmer to the situation. The lieutenant, in turn, blasted a Code Red message to all law officers in the area.

Chigger drove back to the nursery to wait. Within minutes, sheriff's deputies and local policemen surrounded the greenhouse location. Not sure what they would find inside the warehouse, they had arrived without sirens. Stealth mode.

On foot, the officers split up, with a few silently sneaking in the front door. The rest moved in through the back door. Chigger anxiously waited outside by Billy's pickup.

With guns drawn, Lieutenant Swimmer and Officer Williams stepped into the front of the warehouse room along with Sergeant Bowers and Frank Barnes. The remaining force, including men from the sheriff's office, stepped in from the back. They all arrived inside in time to hear Billy scream, "Come and get me, Birdman. I'm not afraid of you."

What the officers saw they couldn't comprehend at first. Billy was tied to an office chair. Sara Cornsilk was strapped down on a hospital gurney. And a very large, menacing black bird was on the floor next to the gurney. The bird flapped its huge wings and rose up off the floor.

The policemen thought the bird had been startled by their arrival and was flying away. But instead, when it had almost reached the rafters, the bird emitted an ear-splitting screech. It dove downward with great speed and was about to attack. It was headed straight for Billy!

It was officer Lacey Williams who got off the first shot. Then, as if startled out of a daydream, the others fired at the diving raven. A volley of shots rang out. Several bullets tore through the bird's body. The ugly beast released a shrill, tormented screech as it tumbled downward. Seconds later, the bird's corpse hit the concrete floor with a loud thud.

Lieutenant Swimmer ran to the raven to make sure it was dead. Officer Williams took care of Sara, undoing the straps and making sure she was okay. Sergeant Bowers untied Billy from the chair.

"Are you all right?" Bowers asked him.

Before Billy could answer, Lieutenant Swimmer yelled, "Get over here. You've got to see this!"

Everyone circled the lieutenant and the dead bird. The bird's body was twisting and changing as it lay on the floor. Its feathers melted away. Its wings morphed into human arms. For a brief moment, they saw Ravenwood, the gym teacher, lying before them.

But the process wasn't complete. Ravenwood's face and hands began aging before their eyes. Seconds later, they saw the shriveled body of a very old American Indian man. In an instant, the old man's eyes popped wide open. There was a look of horror and panic in them. It was as if he just realized the harsh reality of his situation.

His body jerked upward as it began to decay. A ghostly green mist flew up out of that body and floated above them. The mist shortly formed into the shape of a man, an evil man with an evil grin. Then the form shot upward and disappeared.

The whole thing was enough to make your head spin with confusion and awe. Then everyone looked back down at the floor. Mr.

Ravenwood's dead body was lying where the bird and the old Indian had been.

"What the heck just happened?" Swimmer asked, looking at Billy. "Do you know what's going on here?"

"Yeah, sort of," Billy said, still in awe. "But you wouldn't believe it."

Just then they heard a voice call, "Billy? Billy, are you all right?"

They looked around to see Chigger coming into the warehouse.

"Chigger!" Billy exclaimed with excitement. "Boy, am I glad to see you!"

The two old friends hugged and left the warehouse together. Lieutenant Swimmer never got a real answer to his question.

CHAPTER 13
Number Thirteen

A few days later, Grandpa Wesley was released from the hospital. He and the rest of the Buckhorn family were invited to a little celebration at the police station. Chigger and his parents were invited, as were Sara and her family. Of course, Lieutenant Swimmer also asked a couple of newspaper reporters to come so the local police department could get some good publicity.

During the event, Billy and Chigger were given citations for bravery in honor of their actions in the case. They'd helped stop a dangerous child predator before he had a chance to hurt any children in their area.

A more in-depth background check had revealed that Ravenwood had harmed several children among the Eastern Cherokees in

North Carolina. But then he was using the name Raulingwood instead of Ravenwood. So there was no record of the man as he was known in Oklahoma. As an athletic coach in North Carolina, he'd kidnapped and tortured several students.

Sara, who was an attractive sixteen-year-old Cherokee girl, was especially grateful to Billy for his heroism. She approached him near the punch bowl as he chatted with Chigger.

"Billy, I want to thank you for saving me," she said in a low, sweet voice. "If you hadn't rammed your chair into the gurney, there's no telling what that evil thing might have done."

"Ah, it was nothing," Billy replied, a little flustered by the attention from the girl.

"Oh, no," Sara protested. "It was definitely something."

Chigger just watched with amusement as the conversation continued.

"As a matter of fact, my parents and I would like to invite you over for dinner," she said. "We'd like to spend some time with you to get to know you better."

"Well, uh, I guess that'd be all right," Billy replied with a stutter.

Then, unexpectedly, she raised her index finger to her lips and kissed it. Then she placed the kissed finger on Billy's neck, right on top of the spider web scar. Using her other hand, she slipped a piece of paper into his hand. She gave him a big smile and trotted back to her parents. Billy flushed with embarrassment. Chigger took full advantage of the moment.

"Billy's got a girlfriend," he said in a mocking tone.

"Oh, shut up, Chigger," Billy said as he opened the folded piece of paper.

"What does it say? What does it say?" Chigger asked excitedly.

"It's her address and phone number," Billy answered, looking toward Sara, who stood across the room. She winked at him, and again he blushed.

After that, Chigger's parents came over and stood next to Chigger.

"Billy, I want to apologize for listening to those rumors and not trusting you," Chigger's dad said. "We should've known better." He reached out his hand to Billy and they shook.

Chigger's mom gave him a hug and added, "You're welcome at our house anytime."

Then Chigger chimed in. "And I still want to manage your career when the reality TV offers come pouring in," he said with a laugh.

Billy punched his friend in the arm and knew that everything was back to normal. Well, almost everything.

The next day a newspaper story reported some details about the kidnapping of Sara and the death of Mr. Ravenwood. The story reminded readers of Billy Buckhorn's brush with lightning. Then it went on to explain how he'd amazingly prevented the injury of a busload of students. Finally, it praised him for his other accomplishments in saving Mr. Wildcat, his own grandfather, and Sara Cornsilk. The story even mentioned how

Chigger had helped by stumbling onto Ravenwood's hideout. But there was no mention of the strange events that had taken place in the nursery warehouse.

It wasn't long before letters from readers started arriving at the Buckhorn house. One woman wanted Billy to come and touch her car to see if she was going to have an accident. Another woman wanted Billy's help in locating a lost wedding ring. A man asked Billy to help him locate his twin brother who'd gone missing several years ago. An elderly Cherokee lady said she'd pay him to come to her house and rid her of a ghost that haunted the place.

On and on the requests came in. Billy and his dad talked about what should be done with all these requests. They decided it would be best to ask Wesley about that. Wesley was at home healing from his wounds. So Billy and his dad drove to the elder Buckhorn's house so they could see how he was feeling.

The three generations of Buckhorns sat down at Grandpa's kitchen table to drink coffee and talk. Billy showed the stack of letters to Wesley.

"That's how it begins," the elder said. "People hear about your abilities. Maybe they hear about how you helped someone they know. Pretty soon they're lined up outside your house, waiting for you to perform the miracle they need."

"What am I supposed to do?" Billy said. "I can't help these people. I don't even know where to begin."

"I do," Wesley said with a smile. "Your grandma taught me before she died. And, when you're ready, I'll teach you. You already know the basics. You've already experienced the power of the dark side of the medicine. So you know what you're up against."

Billy let that thought sink in for a moment before he spoke again.

"In my vision at the stomp dance, I saw a ladder with thirteen rungs. Why thirteen? I thought that was bad luck."

"Good question," Wesley replied. "I bet your dad knows the answer to that."

"As a matter of fact, I do," Billy's dad said. "The number thirteen came to mean bad luck among European Christians a long time ago. Gatherings of witches, known as covens, numbered thirteen. Friday the thirteenth became unlucky after the Catholic pope had several of his enemies arrested or killed on that day a thousand years ago."

"So it's a European myth?" Billy asked.

"Yep," Billy's dad replied. "But if you think about it, Jesus and his disciples numbered thirteen, so it really doesn't make sense."

"Among us Cherokees and several other tribes, the number thirteen is actually a good thing," Wesley added. "Our old lunar calendar has thirteen months because there are thirteen full moons within a year. And, as you saw in your vision, there are thirteen steps on the ladder of Cherokee spiritual growth. That's when you become a true Human Being."

"Okay, I'm beginning to get it," Billy said thoughtfully. "I have a lot to learn. Like how did Ravenwood get mixed up with the dead medicine man Blacksnake?"

"I'll tell you exactly how that happened," Grandpa said.

He stepped into his bedroom and returned toting a large, old book. It was the book Chigger discovered in Ravenwood's car at the nursery. Wesley placed the book on the kitchen table in front of Billy.

"Go ahead and take a look," the elder instructed.

Billy opened the worn cover and looked at the title page. It was handwritten in the Cherokee alphabet.

"What does it say?" he asked.

"*Cherokee Book of Medicine,*" Wesley answered. "It is an original version of the copied pages I inherited from your great-grandfather. He's the one whose pocket watch you carry."

"I've heard you mention this book," Billy said as he turned the pages. "This is the old record of the Cherokee medicine ways. The magic phrases and sacred words."

"Exactly," Wesley confirmed. "This copy belonged to Benjamin Blacksnake. It was found among Ravenwood's personal belongings."

"How did you get it?" Billy's dad asked.

"Lieutenant Swimmer gave it to me," Grandpa replied. "He said the case was closed and it wouldn't be needed as evidence. Especially since they're pretending they didn't see what they saw in the warehouse."

"How did Ravenwood get hold of it?" Billy asked.

"That's something else the police shared with me," Grandpa answered. "Swimmer said that when Raulingwood moved to the Eastern Cherokee reservation, he lived in an old house where Blacksnake had once lived. I guess Blacksnake's ghost lingered around the house, waiting for some unsuspecting victim to find his medicine book hidden there."

"So it really wasn't Raulingwood, or Ravenwood, who was harming those kids," Billy observed. "Blacksnake had taken over his body and his life."

"That's right. Ravenwood was really a victim too."

"This is all so bizarre," Billy said. "It's hard to believe it's real."

"Oh, it's real, all right," Wesley said. "And it's just the beginning for you, Billy. When I was in the hospital, you stepped up and did what needed to be done. You took the next brave step on the ladder in your vision. On the ladder of your life. The things you'll see and the things you'll do in the future would boggle a normal person's mind."

"Ravenwood called me abnormal," Billy said. "He meant it as an insult."

"You come from a long line of abnormal people," Billy's dad said.

Wesley picked up his cup of coffee and proposed a toast.

"Here's to being abnormal," he said, "And, Billy, may you have a long, abnormal life."

Three generations of Buckhorns clinked their cups together in celebration.

ABOUT THE AUTHOR

Gary Robinson, a writer and filmmaker of Cherokee and Choctaw Indian descent, has spent more than twenty-five years working with American Indian communities to tell the historical and contemporary stories of Native people in all forms of media. His television work has aired on PBS, Turner Broadcasting, Ovation Network, and others. His nonfiction books, *From Warriors to Soldiers* and *The Language of Victory*, reveal little-known aspects of American Indian service in the US military from the Revolutionary War to modern times. He has also written three other teen novels, *Thunder on the Plains*, *Tribal Journey*, and *Little Brother of War*, and two children's books that share aspects of Native American culture through popular holiday themes: *Native American Night Before Christmas* and *Native American Twelve Days of Christmas*. He lives in rural central California.